Treble
DAMAGES

A NOVEL

J. Lynn

Copyright © 2012 by J. Lynn

ISBN-10: 1937705102
ISBN-13: 978-1-93770510-7

Also available in E-book
ISBN-13: 978-1-93770511-4

Library of Congress Control Number: 2012922560

Printed in the United States of America

Books by J Lynn
www.booksbyjlynn.com

Cover Design: Maverick Literary
Cover Photo: Getty Images

Treble DAMAGES

A NOVEL

J. Lynn

Treble
DAMAGES

A NOVEL

J. Lynn

Chapter 1

Sydney Starks
Saturday, June 2002
Malibu, Ca.

I should not have told her. I should have walked out the house without telling her a damn thing. Cole is not going to just let this go. She will drill me like a sergeant. The less she knows the better it will be for all of us. All I know is I cannot be implicated in whatever it is wrong with Cyclone.

True, I gave him the Ecstasy, but I took some with him. I'm perfectly fine. I also did not force him to take that line up his fucking nose, either. He's a grown ass man. I kept telling myself he's in this predicament because of the choices he's made. But I knew deep inside that if anyone found out we were here, we would be blamed.

Fuck!

I lit a cigarette and slowly inhaled the toxic stick, feeling the smoke contaminate my internal organs. Instantly, I was high again, but not too inhibited that I could not think clearly.

I never thought that I would be in a situation like this. Nor have I ever seen anyone go into a seizure. The Cyclone OD'ing was definitely a first. I should have checked his pulse again. But shit, his ass was drooling and foaming at the mouth.

That shit freaked me out. So, I stepped outside on The Cyclone's beach front deck — the slight stir of the wind chilled my bones.

I really fucked up this time. I searched for a makeshift ashtray and found an empty beer bottle on the patio table. I dropped the cigarette butt inside. I collected the remaining bottles and began tidying up the house.

I collected my thoughts; I sure as hell don't want to be caught slipping. I know how Cole thinks and she loves to play attorney. That's why I'm not trying to become involved: I can control my actions. But knowing Cole, she will probably be the problem.

* * *

As I wiped down the kitchen counter, my mind wandered, trying to retrace what went wrong. The night started like any other Saturday night. Cole and I were en route to the Outkast after party at the House of Blues off Sunset Boulevard. My intentions were to meet one of my girls, Kimberly, at The Palm restaurant off Santa Monica Boulevard, drop off her phone that she left at the office, and then head over to the Westin Hotel to meet my play-cousin and business partner, Reggie Woods. Then we would all end the night at the Outkast after party at the House of Blues.

On our way out of the Westin, I felt a slight pull on my arm. I thought it was some clown trying to cop a feel. I was quick to react, ready to curse out the damn fool who dared to lay his hands on me, but instead I locked eyes with Peyton "The Cyclone" Waters.

"You were just going to walk by without speaking?" He flashed me a sexy smile that could melt the edible panties that I wore.

He was a pleasing distraction: a nice fitting baby blue Armani suit and a crisp white open-collar shirt underneath. The colors were smooth against his milk chocolate tone. His diamond encrusted medallion peeked through his shirt revealing Tasmanian Devil spinning into a cyclone. He wore two diamond earrings on his left ear and a large face diamond encrusted watch on his wrist. He also sported the championship ring on his left ring finger.

I gave him a full lingering hug, remembering how well-endowed he was.

"How have you been?" I asked him; it had been four years since we last spoke.

The Cyclone invited me to his table. Because of who he was, one of my favorite groups could wait. He went on to tell me that he had just finalized an endorsement deal with Gatorade and was about to celebrate his up-coming endeavor. Meanwhile, Cole was warding off his teammate Demarco Williams' advances. Demarco was hideous compared to The Cyclone. I did not know what scared me more: his third eye or those horse teeth. A wrong nibble and your nipple would rip in half—I was hardly envious of Cole at that moment.

"So how long has it been?" His tone was sincere. I had always liked that about him. He was always so attentive as if we were the only two that mattered in this crazed out world.

"Too long," I replied.

The Cyclone was in his second year playing in the National Football League. He was drafted out of UCLA in the first round by the San Diego Chargers and was fast becoming an icon. By all measures, his life had been a success story of somebody who had emerged out of the ghetto.

After a couple of dances, we managed to ditch Demarco and followed The Cyclone to his home. He was so high that he thought he could handle both of us in the bedroom. Knowing Cole, she was not going to fuck around on her boyfriend, Kavion Cottrell. She would wait downstairs while I get my kitty stroked.

He led me upstairs to his master suite. The black and gold décor was elegant and grand. Majestic. Like Royalty. His California king-size bed was situated in the center of the room. The four posts were adorned with intricate designs of Africa and Tree of Life; it was quite beautiful.

Taking the lead, I told him to lie down. I pulled off his shoes and his pants. The size and girth of his shaft mesmerized me, and I could not wait to try a sampling. I was hornier than a Catholic school girl at a frat party; however, he was inebriated and I doubted seriously that he would be able to keep it up.

Ah, but he did. It was so memorable. But then I woke up to him shaking uncontrollably. I was horrified by the sight of The Cyclone's body going into convulsions. I did not know whether he was an epileptic and that shit scared the fuck out of me. He was foaming at the mouth and his eyes began to rolling towards the back of his head.

Fuck!

I was hoping this was some hallucination or The Cyclone had a demented sense of humor. No matter how hard I hoped, this was a bad dream. The seizures stopped and he was still breathing—barely—but he still had a pulse.

Reality had set in, and there was no way I'd be calling the cops.

Chapter 2

Cole Kennedy
Saturday, June 2002
Malibu, Ca.

Sydney shook me forcefully. "Cole, Cole . . . Wake up!"

The abrupt reaction caused me to jerk up fast.

"What time is it?" I yawned, tired from the long night of partying. I wiped the sleep from my eyes and the drool that trickled from my mouth.

"It's time to go," she hissed.

Her movements were erratic. First, she walked out of the room screaming "fuck" repeatedly at the top of her lungs. Then she walked over the bar and poured herself a double shot of Patrón silver. She cringed and shook her head as the burning liquid went down her throat. Mindlessly, she poured another shot.

In the three years knowing Sydney, I'd never witnessed her drinking so early in the morning. Nor had I ever witnessed her being so out of control. Gazing aimlessly, Sydney was in another world. She tripped on the area rug, but regained her posture and stumbled past me out onto the large wrap-around deck of Peyton Waters' beach front home. I never met him during his matriculation at UCLA, but his reputation as a ladies' man preceded him. So, it was no surprise that he wanted to bring both Sydney and I back to his place.

Suddenly, Sydney broke down and fell to her knees crying uncontrollably chanting, "No . . . No . . . No!"

Alarmed, I walked out on the deck. I wrapped my arm around her and began rubbing her back. I did not know whether she'd gotten into an argument with The Cyclone or her boyfriend, Jody, but her actions told me it was something worse.

"Sydney, girl, you're scaring me. Tell me what's going on? Did that motherfucker do something to you?" I queried.

"No, it's The Cyclone," she answered between sobs. "I thought I was trippin' but something is really wrong with him."

I pulled her up to her feet so that she could show me what she was talking about. I followed her upstairs to his large master bedroom suite.

"What do you mean what's wrong? Sydney what happened?" I asked.

Peyton was motionless on the bed. His eyes were rolled to the back of his head and was choking on his own vomit. Panic suddenly rushed through my body. I should have left when I had a chance.

I yelled for Sydney to help me turn him to his side, but she just stood there. It took everything within me to turn his two hundred-plus pound muscular body over to the side.

"Sydney, call 911 now!" I barked while I attempted to clear his airway.

"I can't do that, Cole," she said. "They'll think we did this to him and I can't get involved in this . . . I'm sorry . . . I can't go back to jail."

"What in the fuck do you mean you can't go back to jail? This is Peyton, and he needs our help."

I scrambled to find a phone, but Sydney blocked my path by standing in my way.

"Cole, you are not looking at the whole picture. You are in law school. You, of all people, should know what I am talking about. What do you think they will do to us if he dies? Huh, I will tell you what they will do. They will hunt and kill the two hoes that killed their idol, their American dream. "

"What are you talking about?" I reacted. "I had nothing to do with this. The right thing to do is call the cops. Now get out of my way!"

She would not budge.

"Cole Kennedy, listen to me and listen good. I will not be here when the cops come. I am not going back to jail for the rest of my life.

"And what about your career. What would Daddy think when he sees his little girl plastered all over the news for her involvement in death of The Cyclone?"

"Sydney, he's not dead," I said. "Tell me what happened and why we would be held responsible?"

I walked over to the window and peered hopelessly out to the ocean, wishing that I'd never come in the first place. I did not need any involvement with cops especially on this end of the spectrum. This could taint my career as an entertainment lawyer before my career ever begins. I should have been at home dreaming about some righteous loving from my boyfriend, Kavion Cottrell.

She sighed. "I don't know what happened. After we fucked, he said he wanted to rest for a few minutes before round two." She began pacing the floor. "Shit, I don't know what happened because I woke up with him convulsing in the bed like crazy. I thought he might be an epileptic. So I waited for him to calm down but then he just stopped moving."

"How long has he been like this?" I checked his pulse again; it was still faint.

"Maybe thirty minutes before I came down to get you . . ."

After a quick perusal of his place, we gathered our belongings and left through the back door. We backed out of the driveway and drove off. Down the block, I saw a pay phone and made a quick decision to called 911.

After making the call, I sped away without looking into my rear-view mirror, praying The Cyclone would be okay.

Chapter 3

Cole Kennedy
Saturday, June 2002
Los Angeles, Ca.

After I dropped Sydney off at her co-op apartment downtown, I stopped at the supermarket and picked up a bottle of Tylenol and a box of chamomile tea to calm my nerves. I replayed the situation with The Cyclone in my mind during the entire drive home.

I should have done the right thing and stayed with him until the police arrived. Instead, I allowed Sydney to get in my head and cloud my judgment.

I ran a nice hot bath to soak my anxiety away. The song playing on the radio was interrupted for a special announcement that Peyton "The Cyclone" Waters was in intensive care. He'd suffered a massive stroke and was in a coma after an apparent cocaine overdose. I quickly sat upright, swooshing water over the side of the tub. My heart began beating harder and I felt sick. The room spun out of control. I could not believe it. The only thing that kept me sane was the fact that I possibly saved his life.

I did not recall seeing him doing cocaine, so why didn't Sydney disclose this piece of information? After regaining my composure, I finished washing off and immediately dialed Sydney's number.

"Did you hear about Peyton?" I asked as soon as she picked up.

"Yeah, I heard." Sydney sniffled, "I think I need to come by later so we can get our stories straight. I am sure Peyton's friend Demarco will bring us up to the police, if they suspect any foul play. We will be the prime suspects in this whole investigation."

"Why would they suspect foul play? Did you know he took cocaine? "

"Yeah, we snorted a line together before we hooked up." The swallow she took was rather audible. "I don't feel like speaking on this right now. We can talk about this later. I am supposed to pick up Jody from baseball practice since his car is in the shop again. I'll be there in an hour."

Click!

She hung up the phone before I could respond.

* * *

An hour had more than since come and passed. I was beyond angry. This would definitely be the last time I'd allow Sydney to screw up my plans or dictate how I'd spend my Saturday night.

Now, she's talking about us being implicated of wrongdoing. She was the one in his bed. She was the last one with him—I should have listened to my rational side and waited for the EMTs rather than allow Sydney to persuade me otherwise.

Where the fuck is she anyway? I wondered aloud to myself, looking down the street through the sheer white curtains. Furious, I pulled my cell phone out of my black Chanel bag and began dialing her number. She answered on the third ring.

"Where are you? You better be at the hospital, or better yet, stuck on the side of the road because you have a flat tire," I said, pausing long enough to catch my breath. "I thought you said you'd be here going on two hours ago . . . I had to break another night with Kavion just so I could twiddle my thumb wondering if you were coming or not . . . I'm tired of this narcissistic shit from you—"

Sydney Starks was the first female I connected with after moving to Los Angeles a few years ago. I met her at the neighborhood recreation center my first week at jazzercise class, and we have been inseparable ever since.

Sometimes we're so much alike that we could be mistaken for sisters. In reality, though, our upbringing was absolutely different.

I was born and raised in Oakland. Both of my parents were successful in their respective careers. My mother was a tenured professor of anthropology at UC Berkeley, and my father was a renowned plastic reconstructive surgeon. I attended Saint Mary's private school until I begged my parents to allow me to go the nearby public school, Skyline High, for my junior year because I wanted to experience a traditional public school with boys my own age.

Since I can remember, I've traveled abroad each year to a different place. France. Rome. Aruba. Switzerland. Germany. Italy's my favorite place of all.

After graduating from UC Berkeley in sociology, my father was so excited that I was accepted to his alma mater, Stanford, in nearby Palo Alto for grad school. But I couldn't bear to break his heart and that I had already decided to get my juris doctorate at UCLA school of Law.

Whereas I've lived the privileged life, Sydney's was far from privileged. She grew up in South Central Los Angeles' east side. She never knew her father, and her mother was a single parent who introduced Sydney to the world of strippers, sex, and drugs. Despite the fact her mother still strip at a Gentleman's club for a living, Sydney was able to triumph over the statistics by graduating from USC.

Also by the time Sydney had turned twenty-one, she and one of her childhood friends, Reggie Woods, formed a partnership and started a high-end escort service for the rich and famous. I've actually admired how she's become a successful entrepreneur maintaining a clientele base of doctors, lawyers, bankers, movie executives, and professional athletes. It's not something I'm interested in. But if it makes her independent and not hurting anyone in the process, I say do your thang.

Now, I do have a problem with her business partner, Reggie. He's about as grimy and repulsive as they come, and I don't trust him at all. Humph. He propositioned me the first time I met him.

"You have the look my clients would pay top dollar for." His voice was heavy but raspy, reminding me of the New York rapper Jada Kiss.

As if I would stoop to that level. He could kiss my ass. I had to break it down that I was not into that scene, and that my father would disown me if I ever considered doing it even for one night.

"You're my girl and everything but I am tired of you fucking up my weekend," I continued ranting. "I could have been fucking Kavion's brains out instead of fucking around with you."

Laughing, she responded. "Don't worry, I won't be long. I had to handle a few things for Reggie . . . I wouldn't bother you if I didn't think we need to be consistent with our story. I'll be there in two minutes."

She hung up again on me. It bothered me that she wasn't affected by recent events involving The Cyclone.

Annoyed, I called Kavion.

"Hi there," he answered. "I thought you were trying to tell me to fuck off." I could hear him smacking on the other end of the line.

"Not you," I said.

I could not help but muse about the time I spent with Kavion just two nights ago. He showed me a new meaning of being blissfully satisfied. My kitty began pulsating at the memory of being stroked into oblivion. I thought that I would be the one turning him out, but I ended up being the one who went straight to sleep snoring after we finished.

"Have you heard about The Cyclone?" Kavion inquired, smacking into the phone.

Suddenly, I was consumed with remorse. "Yes, I heard . . ." Then I reasoned why should I have any feelings of remorse. I had nothing to do with his current state. I tried saving his life.

"Cole, did you hear me?"

"No, I kind of spaced off there. What happened?"

"I said a few of us are going to the hospital to show Peyton support. You know, he graduated from UCLA last year, and Coach Jackson and a few teammates are shaken up badly. Did you want to come along?"

"No, not really. I have a research paper to work on. You want to hook up later?" I hoped that he would agree.

Guilt began creeping in again. I could not go to the hospital, although I knew I had nothing to do with The Cyclone's current condition.

Chapter 4

Stefan Lewis
Seattle, Washington

I made sure that I parked four cars down the street from Fiona's home. Close enough that I could see her through the open windows, yet far enough that I would not draw too much attention to myself.

I watched her for two solid weeks. I probably knew her fucking routine better than she did. I saw her light blue 1999 Toyota Camry in my rear-view mirror—I pretended to be looking at a map when she passed by.

She'd turn into her driveway at exactly six-thirty in the evening. I knew by seven-thirty she'd be sipping on her second glass of Chardonnay, and she'd be in the bathtub by eight.

Today should be perfect for what I have in store for Fiona. Her betrayal was unforgivable. She slept with the enemy. My arch nemesis. I sat there watching and waiting. Waiting for the time to make my move.

"I hate her ass," I mumbled under my breath as I pulled my Seattle Mariners baseball cap over the reddish brown wig I purchased at the costume store a few weeks ago.

Meanwhile, I entertained myself by recalling the time when we were happy and in love. I remembered when we first met as if it were yesterday: Her eyes drew me into her soul. Also, just one seductive look from her always had me wanting to ravish her body with the intensity of two lovers reunited for only one night.

The scent of the bouquet of lilies that I had in my car reminded me how sweet her pussy tasted just before making love to her. How I took pleasure in satisfying all of her pleasure spots. And by that, I learned how to master the art of sucking and eating pussy.

She once confided in me that I was the first to make her climb walls of delirium. She said she never had a man who could match the same intensity as her vibrator. I loved how her face contorted while she bit her bottom lip. Even sexier was her eyes rolling to the back of her skull as she gripped my head like she palmed a basketball.

It was as if she invited me to devour every drop of her sweet crème flavored nectar. She made me feel as if I mastered tempting and seducing her mind and body before giving her nine inches of additional euphoria.

Shit!

My train of thought was broken by Mrs. Wannamaker — Fiona's next door neighbor — as she shuffled down the street with King, her yellow but supposedly white poodle. I always got a kick out of watching how owner and mutt sported wild hair-dos, as if by the grace of God both survived being struck by lightning.

So, I waited until Mrs. Wannamaker closed the door before executing my perfect revenge. As soon as she turned off the porch light, I pulled down the visor and admired myself once more—I was amazed how much a wig and fake mustache could alter my image. I looked nothing like myself.

Fiona wouldn't be able to recognize me even if I stood at her door with only a bow tie and a smile. I smoothed my mustache firmly in place for the final time. I adjusted the baseball cap making sure that I hid my grey eyes, if by chance there were any witnesses.

My heart pounded so hard that it felt as if it would burst. I needed to calm down fast. This is not the time to have an attack.

"God I hate her ass," I hissed.

When I get like this, the Pranayama breathing technique is the only thing that's ever calmed me down. So, I practiced the yoga breathing technique and concentrated on my task at hand. Humph, I wondered what would be her excuse for cheating this time. It won't matter because any apologies would be too late.

I said a small prayer as I exited the car. Although most nights Fiona's neighborhood was quiet, tonight felt surreal. It was as if the briskness of the wind had whistled an "it's time" message into my ear. That had to be the sign from God.

I walked over to the passenger side and was careful to remove the flower vase without crushing any petals. I felt even more confident knowing that this would be the perfect way to end our relationship. I want to make a statement and I want it to be poetic.

What Fiona never understood was that she drove me to a place where I vowed that if I ever got there I'd never return. The monster within always finds a way to surface even when I've found that I could control myself.

I was desperate for her affection. So desperate for our love to work that I overlooked a lot of her shit. And when I found out she was seeing someone else behind my back, I knew deep inside that I lost her. Once she crossed the line of unfaithfulness, I could never trust her again. Then I found out about her engagement to LaSalle Blalock. First, that sent me into depression. Now I'm just full of hatred.

She was supposed to marry me, not LaSalle. She's hurt me for the last time. I cannot fathom the idea of some other guy touching the love of my life. The mere thought of her infidelity has made it impossible to breathe. But her luck won't be as fortunate.

As I approached the steps of Fiona's cottage style home, I closed my eyes again for a quick prayer, hoping that I wouldn't fuck this up. Then I paused for several seconds knowing once I ring the doorbell there would be no turning back. Whatever happens will be determined by Fiona.

"Who is it?" she asked, as she got closer.

The sound of her voice irritated the hell out of me. She should be as devastated as I am over the demise of our relationship. Instead, the tone of her voice was as if she could not care how our relationship was ending. If she thinks so little of our relationship, then the hell with her.

Disguising my voice, I responded, "Last Chance Flowers." I have a delivery. The card says it's from "Salle…"

A deep shooting pain began in my chest and ended at the tip of my limp dick. Her reaction as she fumbled to open the door just sealed her fate. For a split second, I entertained the thought of just killing her as soon as she opened the door. But I'm going to maintain my cool because I have other plans for Miss Fiona Carter.

"Oh these are lovely. LaSalle always knows what I like," she reacted, taking the flowers from my hands.

The sweet smell of her perfume evoked a sensation I promised myself that I would not succumb to. My hand grazed lightly against her soft manicured hand. I savored the touch but only for a moment.

If I had enough nerve, I would be willing to take her back and forgive her for cheating on me, if only it was someone other than LaSalle.

I stared intently at her admiring her beautiful features for the last time. No more dates no more late I figure meet him night walks on the beach dreaming of our future together, or the kinky sex in the park after an early morning jog.

She inhaled the fragrant scent of the lilies as I glanced at my watch. I always timed my work. This is what I called the climax before I go for the kill. Predictably, and like most women I've known, she turned her back on me. If only she knew what a mistake she just made.

"I'll be right back," she said, walking towards the sofa where her purse was.

So vulnerable. So helpless.

Searching through her purse, she pulled out a black wallet. "I want to give you a few dollars for your troubles coming here," she said.

My troubles were with her. If she could have only been faithful, I might have forgiven her.

She invited me to come inside. As I crossed the threshold, I took the latex gloves out of my pocket and began putting them on. I reached back and closed the door behind me, making sure the dead bolt was secure.

Her back still towards me, I took out the bottle of chloroform I found earlier at the university's chemical lab. I carefully poured the chloroform on a handkerchief. This was going to be a bittersweet ending, but I'm not the cause of this pain. She's had no one to blame but herself because she turned her back on what could have been.

Chapter 5

Stefan Lewis
Seattle, Washington

I watched Fiona's ample and ripe booty. I took a mental picture of it. I'm going to miss that pretty booty. I'm going to miss how she made love to me, and how she moved that booty up and down left to right.

Bouncing. Flexing. Bumping. Grinding. She was definitely gifted. I'll miss how she'd mount me reverse cowgirl, allowing me to enjoy the view of her soft but tight ass. She would flex her PC muscles while slowly gliding up and down my dick in a stronghold so tight that it was as if she would break it in half if she moved the wrong way.

I checked my watch again and began a mental countdown. Ten. Nine. Eight . . . Just being this close to her after all we've been through has been so emotional.

Seven. Six. Five . . . I hate her for cheating on me, but I still love her and still want to be with her.

Four. Three. Two . . . Sensing my presence, she turned around and realized that I was only a couple of feet away. I wished that I had a camera to capture the look she just given me. It was a keeper.

One . . . Without mouthing a single word, I edged closer towards Fiona, who began taking steps backwards. Her eyes widened as she lost her balance stumbling over the table and back against the wall facing me. Then I lunged at her and forced the handkerchief over her mouth, pinning her against the wall.

She tried prying my hands away; however, the effect from the chloroform was taking over. Her small frame was of no resistance. Within seconds, I gently laid her on the floor and watched her drift to sleep.

I made my rounds around her home, checking the windows and doors and making sure the telephone went straight to voice mail. On my way back to check on my cheating lover, I admired how she maintained a nice home. She had vibrant abstract art on the light blue walls. She had a small collection of metal and glass sculptures in the living room. I guess she did not have much of a green thumb since all the plants and flowers were artificial. Overall, there was a sense of order, balance and harmony. I would not have expected anything less.

When she came to, the look of confusion was priceless. I'd already carried her up to her bedroom, placed her in bed, and tied her hands in back with Velcro handcuffs. There was no way that she'd be able to free herself. Nonetheless, she appeared unsure whether she was in some weird dream or if the nightmare that she experienced was real. But seeing me, she realized that her dream was real and her world was fucked. Or so it seemed.

"You can have anything you want. My fiancé plays for the Seattle Seahawks," she said. "If its ransom you want, he'll pay it. Just please don't hurt me."

I looked at her incredulously. This bitch had to be kidding me. As if I could be bought with monetary goods from her douche bag loser boyfriend?

She had the audacity to act as though we were never together or had ever known me. As if any of the passionate nights we shared meant nothing to her. I was more than tempted to walk over to the bed and slap her ass.

"What do you want from me?" she queried. "I'll do whatever you ask."

"I bet you will," I mumbled.

I had already decided that I was going to make her squirm and beg for mercy. "What do I want from you? Are you fucking kidding me, Fiona? After all the shit we've been through you're going to treat me like you don't even know me?"

She had a blank expression. "I'm sorry, I just . . . I didn't mean to betray you. If you let me go, I can help you."

"You should have thought of that before you messed around, Fiona. If only you were the woman I thought you were supposed to be."

As I stood over her, she now had the look of a lost puppy nobody wanted. Her eyes were so sad. It was a look that could have killed me. Yet she still did not recognize who was in front of her. She's forcing me to show her the consequences of being a slut.

Her breathing began to quicken, evoking an erotic sensation between my legs. Here I was, less than a foot away from her. Close enough to smell the faint aroma of the wine that she consumed only minutes before I arrived. But there's no way that I was going to give her that visual pleasure.

"I would have given you the world, even killed a motherfucker for you, Fiona," I ranted. "Instead of giving our love a chance to grow into something seismic, you betrayed me by seeing someone else behind my back, making a mockery of me."

She attempted to chortle; she also shook her head in apparent disbelief.

"But who's laughing now?" I was quick to retort. "You will suffer for making me look like a damn fool!"

"Why are you doing this to me?"

"No, how could you do this to me!"

My emotions were now getting the best of me. I found myself pacing back and forth. She's just like all the rest. Only out for herself. And once she gets what she wants, she just tosses you with all the other losers.

"What did I do to you?"

"Are you kidding me?" I yelled. "You should be answering that question for me!"

Furious, I jerked her from lying on the bed to an upright position and shook her. I also gestured as if I would slap her.

"Please don't hurt me," she protested.

"This is all your fault. If you just had . . ."

"If I just had what?"

I shook her again and pushed her back down. "We were supposed to have had a good life together. We were supposed to be a family. How do you expect me to explain this to mother? She was so excited when I announced our engagement." I began pacing back and forth thinking about how this would kill my grandmother, the woman who raised me as her own.

Her eyes began welling with tears. Her lip began to quiver. Perhaps the menacing glare that I just given her finally resonated.

"I'm sorry for whatever it is you said I've done to you."

"It's a little too late for that," I answered, positioning myself directly in front of her. "You made your bed, so now I'm forcing you to lie in it."

She tried sitting up. "I don't know what you're talking about. I don't even know you. Maybe you're confusing me with someone else."

The nerve of her. "Fiona Carter, you know me. You graduated in 2000 from the University of Washington with me. You don't remember we had chemistry together? That's when we met."

"I, uh . . ."

I placed a vanity chair next to her bed and sat down in it. Then I explained, "You and I were supposed to be soul mates. We professed our love to one another after you were crowned homecoming queen. Don't you remember?"

She returned a blank expression. I know I hadn't shaken her so hard that she now had amnesia. Pissed, I stood up and kicked the chair to the side.

"That really bothers me, Fiona. I took our relationship seriously. I paid attention to you. I worshipped the ground you walked. I protected you when you needed me. I was there when it counted the most, not LaSalle.

"Why would you choose him over me? Why couldn't you love me the way I loved you?"

I paused long enough to let that statement sink in. Suddenly, I realized that she was not worth my time or dedication. She did not deserve someone like me. Annoyed by that reality, I pulled the cloth and bottle of chloroform from my pocket.

"Sir, I think you're confusing me with someone else. I'm engaged and plan to be married next week." She began crying. "Please do not do this to me. Just let me go, please—"

I shook my head, showing pity. "If you had only played by the rules, we would not be in this situation. We would have been perfect together."

I glanced down at what was in my possession. Then I made eye contact with her.

"I cannot let you run off with him. Life would have been much simpler if you had only played by the rules."

She shook her head in protest. "Please don't . . ."

"Don't what?" I reacted. "I wish things were different between us, Fiona. But all you did was stomp on my heart. You really hurt me this time, and I cannot forgive you."

I paused for greater impact. I paused for greater impact. Her eyes were a picture of fear.

"It didn't have to end this way, Fiona. You betrayed me and I can't stand for you to go away with him," I continued.

Now my emotions were getting the best of me. I was on the brink of tears. Of all the women I ever dated, Fiona was definitely worth fighting over. Or so I thought. She turned out to be just like all the rest.

"I don't understand," she babbled. "What did I do wrong?"

"You pushed me away; therefore, you've left me with no other choice. You chose someone else over me."

She began sobbing uncontrollably—I rolled my eyes up to the sky.

"It's a little too late for that, Fiona. You had your chance to prove your love to me. Instead, you've proven how much of a slut you really are."

I began to laugh as I covered her nose and mouth with the deadly toxin. She struggled hard to get free from her bed. She tried everything in her power to prevent me from getting closer. But I grabbed her by the neck, forcing her to remain still. As she cried, she fought, bit and kicked me; her feistiness was one of the qualities that I loved most—to the bitter end.

Chapter 6

Cole Kennedy
August 2002
Los Angeles, Ca.

After two months on life support, the doctors pronounced The Cyclone brain dead. His mother made the heart-wrenching decision to pull the plug. He managed to live on his own for only a couple of hours before he succumbed to cardiac arrest.

I was distraught and stricken with guilt after finding out about The Cyclone's death. But these were emotions that Sydney should be feeling. Making matters even worse, instead of attending his memorial, she was entertaining a high roller on the Las Vegas Strip. I could no longer be around someone like her, and I decided to distance myself from her.

It was times like these when I wished I had my mother, Sabrina, around to talk with. But she died in a car accident during the spring semester of my senior year in high school. Whenever I see my father, Darius, I'm always reminded of the cause of her death: she died in a car accident caused by my father's mistress, Terri Malone.

Although my father was also in the car, he survived the accident with both his legs broken, a broken pelvis, two cracked ribs, and a punctured lung. He also sustained a cut from below his left ear down to his chin as a physical reminder. Karma's a bitch and a motherfucker; his dick literally fucked his life over.

For his age, my father's quite handsome. He's tall, lean, and fit. When I think of my father, I see him as the blueprint for Julian McMahon's character Christian Troy from Nip/Tuck. He's a narcissist by nature, which always made him appear cocky and arrogant. He has golden brown eyes just as I have, and he's always worn his hair in a close fade.

While growing up, I had heard countless stories about my father's extramarital affairs. Basically, any pretty bimbo in a skirt was fair game for him. He didn't care if she was twenty-two or fifty-two. There were only two requirements: she had to be pretty and petite.

He had that in my mother. But both my parents were consumed with their careers that neither had any time for each other. Apparently, my father was the one who felt neglected and found satisfaction in the arms and beds of other women. I don't know if my mother chose to ignore the rumors or she was blindly in love. No matter how many times my father strayed, he always came home at night.

Then he fucked up.

Terri Malone walked into my father's practice for breast augmentation and left with my father finding pleasure between her legs. As their relationship progressed, she became demanding. She wanted him to decide either he would leave his family or leave her the hell alone. She actually believed that my father would divorce my mother and marry her. She thought because she was young and beautiful that she had control of my father's mind below the waist.

That's where her plan backfired and she was mistaken. She didn't read the manual my father helped write, "Leave

Them with Their Legs in the Air." She was nothing more than eye candy, a toy my father played with whenever boredom struck. Besides, if my father ever thought about leaving my mother, he would have lost everything he owned.

For months after their break-up, Terri harassed and stalked my father until he was forced into filing a restraining order. That pissed her off even more. She retaliated by plastering flyers all over our neighborhood that he fathered her child and refused to take care of both of them—all lies.

"Dr. Darius Kennedy is not someone you can trust," one side read. "He's manipulative and treacherous. He's irresponsible. Just ask me and his child, Darren Kennedy."

On that fateful night in April 1995, my parents were returning home from a benefit dinner in Palo Alto when a Ford Explorer t-boned their Cadillac STS at an intersection. My mother died at the scene. My father, who was not wearing a seat belt, was ejected from the vehicle and landed on his head. The SUV swerved into oncoming traffic and plowed into an eighteen-wheeler fuel truck, bursting into flames. The driver was burned beyond recognition. It was not until my father came home from the hospital nearly three months after the accident when we learned that the driver and person responsible for the accident was identified as his mistress.

My father was in a coma for twenty-five days; however, he has no memory of what happened before or during the accident. Because of the brain trauma he suffered, he's not capable of processing any emotions.

Physically, we were first apprised by doctors that my father might not ever walk or talk again. But by all accounts, he's made a miraculous recovery. Through intense physical therapy that lasted nearly a year, he was able to regain the ability to do simple things like feeding himself or walking.

Unlike before, though, he's unable to walk with the same swagger or bravado. In other words, he's also experienced sporadic recurrences of lost feeling below the waist, which I've overheard him say, affect his sexual functions.

My father did not lose any long-term memory, which could have affected his vast knowledge of plastic reconstructive surgery. Thus, he's able to work a limited schedule. His practice is comprised of offices in San Francisco, Sacramento, and San Jose, and they continue to thrive.

Most days, my father's recovery has been no consolation for me. My bother Marquise and I lost our mother because of my father's extramarital affairs. I've since battled with bouts of depression knowing that my father's lifestyle was largely responsible for my mother's death. I still harbor bitter feelings of betrayal and resentment because if he had only kept his dick in his pants my mother would still be alive today. And for that, a part of me will always hate him.

Since he has no memory of the accident, I've made it a point of reminding him why my mother died. "Each time you see that scar on your face, and whenever you lose any feeling below your waist, that's your reward for cheating on my mother," I've told him. "Her death is your fault."

"I can't bring back your mother," he's often tried telling me. "I'm only human. Eventually, we have to move on. I have to, no matter how painful it is, although I can't really feel it most of the time."

Just thinking about him pisses me off. I often find myself sulking and having headaches. And why did I get myself involved with Sydney?

Chapter 7

Cole Kennedy
Los Angeles, California

The Kappa fraternity hosted an end-of-the-summer barbecue and pool party at one of its frat houses in Ladera Hills. I wasn't in much of a partying mood since Kavion was still in Georgia with his family.

His trip there was unexpected. His mother fell down a flight of stairs and broke her leg. Not only did he drop everything, we had to cancel our trip to Cancùn, Mexico. Instead of seven days on the beaches of Cozumel overlooking the deep green water, snorkeling, and exploring other possibilities, he returned home to help with the family restaurant. He promised me he would make it up to me once he returned.

So, here I am at this place and my gut instinct's telling me that I should have driven to this party in my own car. But I still had a two-hour drive to see Marquise compete in his last martial arts tournament in San Diego before he was to be deployed by the Navy.

I glanced down at my watch. It was one-thirty the morning. I tried finding my sorority sisters Charisma and Shanté who brought me here. They're nowhere to be found. That left me searching every possible place of this five-thousand square foot home. But it did not help that people were everywhere—the main gathering areas, along every wall, up and down the stair cases, the swimming pool, and Jacuzzi.

I tried calling Charisma and Shanté on my cell phone and both calls went straight to voice mail. Damn. Now I began feeling stranded.

Concerned, I went outside and searched for Shante's Honda Accord. It was not where I recalled us parking. I would not have left my sisters under any circumstance. Now they've really pissed me off.

Just to be certain, I checked my phone to confirm whether I missed any calls from Charisma or Shanté. There were no calls from them.

Why would they leave without telling me?

It was an uncomfortable walk back inside the mansion. I recalled seeing Barry, a frat brother whom I knew, playing spades on the deck. I was reduced to hoping he could give me a ride. I grabbed a bottle of Corona and made my way to him.

"That's right, count 'em up?" he exalted after a winning play in dominoes. "Y'all don't know who you're messing with."

"Shut up, bitch. You just got lucky," one of the players retorted to Barry.

"Ain't no luck here."

He happened to look up and recognize me. "Hey, Cole. Don't worry about a thing. I gotcha."

"What do you mean, you got me?" I delayed taking a sip from the bottle.

"Taking you home," he said, leaning back. He then looked to his right, then left, surveying the table. "This won't take long teaching these amateurs a very important life lesson. Then I'll take you back to your place."

All I could do was shake my head. My sorority sisters had left me at this party and I was to be taken home by Barry, whom I only knew because I had tutored him in Chemistry two semesters ago. He had been dating another of my sorority sisters, Kendra.

"Okay, I guess I better sit and watch. I don't feel like mixing and mingling anymore."

Barry's ego seemed to inflate by a few pounds knowing that he had a female in his presence. "Yeah, you do that." He picked up his dominoes and slammed one on the table. "That's two [ten points], damnit!"

Then he looked over at me, smiling. "Cole, why don't you keep score?"

True to form, Barry must have been feeling it the entire time as literally talked shit before each turn he took, and he scored at will on his three opponents. It almost seemed comical by the way he frustrated all of them with his playing strategy.

Afterward, I joked, "Where was that kind of talent when I was tutoring you for Chemistry?"

He shook his head. "I'm just not wired up for that kind of shit. If I didn't need the class, I wouldn't have taken it. But look here. Charisma and Shante went back to your place with a couple of fellas, and they asked me to give you a ride home." He then asked if it would be all right if a couple of his friends came with us since it was late.

"Look, I don't care as long as I get back home," I answered. "I need to be somewhere in the morning, and all I want to do is get some sleep."

"No problem."

When I walked through the door of our apartment accompanied by Barry and his friends, the sounds of Ginuwine's "So Anxious" blared through the CD player, the lights were dimmed, and the smell of black love incense burnt my nostril.

I flick the light switch on. Immediately, I recognized why I was stranded: Charisma and Shanté each were entertaining a male companion in the living room.

I was not going to get into a yelling match with neither of them, although I still wanted to rip into their asses for leaving me hanging. Besides, I was not in the mood to bitch anyone out since it was going to be yet another night where everybody would be getting some loving except me.

Shanté, cozy on the love seat with her boyfriend-of-the-month Rome, was the first to notice me.

"Hey, girl, I'm sorry about leaving you, I couldn't find you and then I ran into Barry . . . Well, you know how I get when I'm horny."

"Uh-huh, tell me anything," I snapped back at her.

Rome was too embarrassed to look up. It didn't really matter, anyway, because I knew later I just might get my dose of late-night comedy when she's screaming at the top of her lungs that he's laying the pipe deep inside her.

Talk about massaging someone's fragile ego?

By the time I pulled off my jacket, hung it up, and closed the closet door, Charisma and her date were headed towards the stairs—she was being tugged at the hand by a tall and sexy mocha complexioned guy that I'd never seen before.

This was not right at all.

"Cole, I'd like to introduce Vinson to you." He extended his hand out to me, eyeing me in a seductive way.

"Nice to meet you," I replied, taking my hand back quickly. He was definitely a hottie and someone I'd be interested in, but he still was not my Kavion.

"Sorry about us leaving you," she said before she leaned forward and whispered into my ear, giggling. "You know I'm about to get my brains fucked out of me."

"Uh-huh, well you know this is going to cost you a stack of your blueberry pancakes," I whispered back to her.

It also dawned upon me that she was a bit tipsy as she weaved while standing in place. "Come on Vinson . . . We've got tonight. Who needs tomorrow?" she tried serenading to him.

And with that, he smiled and walked awkwardly with her up the staircase. She could barely keep herself upright as she missed a step and tripped onto the carpet. She broke her fall with her hands and knees, prompting me to laugh at her.

"You just mind your fucking business," Charisma slurred to me.

"Don't worry about me!"

* * *

I excused myself from Barry and his friends while I changed into something more comfortable—my favorite lounge wear, a faded grey t-shirt, some sweat pants, and fuzzy socks.

When I returned, Barry and his friends Jamil and Anthony were already sitting at the kitchen table playing a hand of dominos. Sometimes, I've felt as though he had become so much of a permanent fixture in our place that my roommates wanted to charge him rent. I also felt that he always wanted to hang out longer than he should whenever he'd come visit.

"Aren't you going to keep score for us, Cole?" he asked.

"No," I retorted.

"That's all right, beautiful," he said, winking at me. "Watch this."

I happened to make eye contact with him and he grinned at me. There was nothing extraordinary about his looks, being that he was brown complexioned with a medium build.

At best, he might be six feet tall. Besides, I always regarded him as a little brother because of the connection we made through my tutoring him.

He seemed to enjoy trying to hold my attention in front of his friends. Next, he peered down at his hand and picked out a domino. As if he were using a judge's gavel, he cocked back, and slammed the domino onto the table.

"Y'all can't fuck with me!" he bragged. "See, Cole, you should be taking score for me."

"Shut the fuck up," Anthony snapped at Barry, exposing the gaudy gold grill in his fucking mouth; he would be better served getting his crooked teeth fixed.

"Why don't you just play before we bounce," announced Jamil.

Of all the people, I was actually shocked that Jamil had anything to say. Whereas Barry and Anthony were loud and outgoing, always into shit, and craving to be at the center of attention, Jamil was their antithesis, being the quiet and loner type.

In my short acquaintance of him, I'd never seen him with any women, although he was incredibly gorgeous. He reminded me of Prince with his light complexion, high cheek bones, and long, wavy hair.

"Yeah, why don't you guys finish your game and bounce," I bantered.

My comment seemed to pique Jamil's curiosity in a strange way. It was as if his hazel colored eyes locked in onto me like radar and he undressed me. Perhaps he had good reason. After all, I'm five-eight, and I have forty D breasts as well as forty-inch hips and an apple bottom, and my warm-up suit did little to hide a couple of my better attributes.

Then again, I could not have cared less about any other man because I was faithful and devoted to Kavion. So I dismissed his eyeballing me and walked over to the refrigerator for a carton of orange juice.

"Gimme fifteen, motherfucker!" Anthony announced after he slammed his domino; he then looked over at Barry, who seemed unfazed.

"I told you that I won second place at a tournament in Reno just two weeks ago." Barry slammed another domino on the table. "Ante up, punk asses!"

This really must have been Jamil's night. He surprised me again with his reaction, a groan. Apparently, Barry's play had blocked any options Jamil had. He was forced to pull dominoes from the stack.

"Uh-huh, that's right. Next time, I'll bring flea collars for both you dog asses!" He looked up at me, smiling once again. "Get ready, beautiful. We'll be playing doubles real soon."

"Give me a minute and I'll be right back," I answered.

Once I reached the upstairs, I heard stifled moans and the headboards bumping against the wall from both rooms—I was even startled by what sounded like someone's ass cheeks being slapped.

Oh, that's right. Hit it hard, baby!

In the other room, I heard some giggling and some light conversation. Damn, this was a night I really wished Kavion was here. I could have had what Charisma and Shanté were having, respectively.

Sighing, I contemplated calling Kavion and having a quick round of phone sex. I could let him know how much I miss him and help myself go to sleep. The only reason why I didn't was because of the three-hour time difference. It would be almost 6 a.m. in Georgia, and I know that Kavion's also a very deep sleeper. He would not flinch even if a bomb was detonated outside.

So, I put on my double crossover sweat shirt and headed back downstairs to the kitchen. "Okay, just one hand. I have to be on the road in a few hours," I announced upon sitting at the table; Jamil had just finished shuffling the dominoes.

"Cole, it's gonna be me and you against Dumb and Dumber," Barry joked.

Anthony shot a quick glare at Barry and shook his head. "I done told you about that shit!" Then he slammed the double-six domino onto the table.

I never played dominoes until attending college. But I'd like to think that I had become competent rather quickly—at least in my opinion. When playing doubles, my philosophy has always been to go for the quick and easy scoring opportunities like this one. I placed a six-three domino on the table, calling out my count of fifteen.

"See, that's what I'm talking about, partner!"

Jamil shook his head and slammed a double-three domino. After studying his hand for several moments, Barry cocked his hand, slammed a six-four domino, and leaned forward looking in Anthony's direction.

"That's ten, pussy!" Then he caught himself, but it was too late.

"Think of this place like your mother's house," I reacted.

"I said I was sorry, partner—"

"Yeah, you need to respect people's shit," Anthony joined in on the banter. "That's why your ass is going to go to the dog pound on your next play. Watch what I'm saying!"

Barry mentioned that he brought a fifth of Southern Comfort from the frat party with him. "Cole, would you get me a glass and some ice?"

I looked up at him, hinting with the glare in my eyes that I was not his maid.

"Please?"

"That's more like it."

"Thank you."

"Better yet," I suggested. "You're here all the time. Why don't you get your own glass? You know where the ice is."

Seconds later, Barry returned with two glasses of Southern Comfort. "I remember how you like it as well."

He was right. It always reminded me of licorice, and the ice always helped it to go down easier. I took a couple of long sips while we continued playing. But it was not long before I began feeling dizzy.

"Cole, it's your turn," Anthony said.

"Yeah, yeah. Sorry. I think because I haven't eaten too much and it's very late."

The next thing I realized the room started spinning, and I could not get up from my seat. I tried to speak but my mouth was dry as cotton balls. I asked Barry to get me a glass of water and turn up the air conditioner.

Moments later, Barry and Anthony helped me over to the sofa.

"Are you sure you're okay?" Barry asked; he appeared sincerely concerned about my well-being.

"I think so. I think I just need to lie down for a while."

Barry sat next to me, placing his arm across my shoulder. I also felt him lightly stroking my hair and the softness of his lips on my forehead.

The last thing that I recalled was Barry telling me how much that he loved me.

"Don't worry," he said before I blanked out. "I'll take real good care of you."

Chapter 8

Stefan Lewis
Seattle, Washington

From the beginning, LaSalle was jealous of my relationship with Fiona. He made it his mission to make my life a living hell. Juvenile pranks. Immature acts. He even pulled down my pants, exposing my family jewels to everyone in the weight room, and embarrassed me in front of a bunch of cheerleaders. It was a dubious moment that followed me over the next two semesters.

"Don't you think that was a bit sophomoric?" I remembered asking him.

"Shut up, fool!"

"This isn't high school, you know?"

"You're right. It isn't." He began laughing and breaking into a song; he never knew me by my name. "This is just the best time of my life. That's why I'm laughing, and you're not."

One of these days, I hissed to myself.

At the time, I still had Fiona. She was my solace and joy. She was what made my time in college worth the while and pass by faster, although I never tried bothering her with my struggles with LaSalle. She noticed me. She accepted me. She opened up to me in ways others never considered.

I knew it was meant to be from the very first time when she asked for my notes and flashed her beautiful smile—it quickly became one of the most important treasures in my life. There was a hint of innocence in the way she did it. Her eyes were bright and mesmerizing. She wore her hair in a high pony tail, bringing focus to her high cheek bone structure. The dimple on her left cheek was so inviting to poke.

"You're such a sweet person," she told me; I was frozen in time and space. "Thank you so much!"

"No, thank you," I stammered.

From that moment forward, it was as though Fiona and I were inseparable. That was until she fell for LaSalle and betrayed me as she did.

I suppose I had every reason to be cursing myself and wanting to be like him. After all, he was our school's star wide receiver. Scouts from several National Football League teams attended all of his games.

Away from the football field, he had more personality and style than at least half of the football team. He'd lived a life where people catered to him since puberty, walking around as if he were the biggest of men on campus. Needless to say, it always seemed that pussy flocked to him like tricks to their pimps.

Consequently, she reneged on our love to be with, of all people, my worst enemy. He had not only violated what was mine, he also defiled what I had and made it worthless.

God only knows how deep my hatred is towards him!

"Tell LaSalle what really happened. Tell him how you had given your heart to me, and me only!" I sneered at her. "Tell him how you appreciated somebody who accepted you as you were just as you had accepted me as I was!

"Tell him . . . Oops, I guess you can't right now. You'll never be able to claim you were some victim in all of this!"

That's because she was like all of the rest. I should not have allowed myself to be fooled by the outward appearance. I should have looked deeper.

And with that, I went ahead and prepared her bathtub with a warm bubble bath. I also lit the red candles that she had surrounding it. I'm sure this was what she would have done had I not showed up. Maybe she would have been thinking about that son of a bitch LaSalle. Maybe, just maybe, she may have allowed my name to cross her mind.

But who's fooling who?

"You pushed me away; therefore, you've left me with no other choice. You chose someone else over me."

Afterward, I returned to her bedroom and carefully undressed her. Almost immediately, I began entertaining some unusually mischievous thoughts. Now I understood why and how some people do get off on fucking people in their sleep. They just seem so inviting. But doing something like that would have defeated everything that I had planned.

It was still a site to behold, carrying her naked body in my arms for the last time. Her head rested so naturally on my shoulders. It was equally surreal and sobering because it reminded me of the last time we shared an intimate and passionate experience. In some of my most personal moments, I often recalled how her walls contracted and relaxed around my pulsating member, which also sent a torrent of release inside of her.

I kissed her forehead and cheek. Then I placed her in the tub, causing the water to splash onto the floor. I pulled the towel from the rack next to the mirror and used it to dry the bathroom tile.

Save the emotions for later, I kept reminding myself. She can no longer hurt you anymore. It was her decision to cheat.

Determined to see this to its conclusion, I sat atop the toilet seat and watched Fiona slip into permanent slumber. She drifted away drifted away in the stillness of the evening. It appeared even the candles acknowledged her departure as they seemed to sway and bow silently before her.

I collected my belongings and wiped away any DNA evidence that even hinted that I was ever there.

"Goodbye, my love," I said, heading out of the bathroom. "I told you if I can't have you, nobody will . . . See you again in another lifetime."

I began contemplating that maybe I could start over fresh. A new start is what I needed. Seattle brought nothing but pain and misery. Maybe a change in weather could change my outlook on life. Maybe moving to Southern California could bring sunshine into my life. With my credentials, a job would not be hard to find in Los Angeles.

And since Fiona's no longer with us, Los Angeles doesn't look so bad after all.

Chapter 9

Cole Kennedy
Los Angeles, Calif.

I fell asleep with Kavion on my mind. After UCLA's victory win over rival USC, a group of us decided to unwind at one of the nearby bars by playing pool and relaxing with a few drinks.

I was so proud of my baby Kavion, who's a star cornerback for the Bruins. He intercepted three passes, including one that was the winning touchdown. He looked so damn good out there that he had me wanting to jump onto the field, tackle him, and beg him to fuck me anyway that he desired.

Before getting out the car, I reminded him that we were not staying long because we had our own private victory party to attend.

We were not there long before a few female groupies made a fool of themselves by throwing themselves at him. That quickly got on my last nerves. Now, I don't mind a little innocent flirting every now and then. It's actually a turn-on for me knowing that another woman finds my man attractive. Conversely, I also know how conniving and scheming some women can be when they think the girlfriend is not watching his every move. And this was one night that I was not sharing a single ounce or inch of Kavion's delicious dick. This was to be his lucky night.

So, I began giving him hints. "You know I like sucking the meat off its bone." That was after I had stuffed a chicken wing in my mouth and pulled out a completely clean bone. After giving him a seductive stare, I was slow to take a sip from my lemonade. "This feels good going down my throat—"

I actually shivered at the thought as the coldness of the drink overcame me.

The message caused a few stares from the guys and a couple of eye rolls and snarling of upper lips from their girlfriends and the unattached groupies. Kavion himself soon reacted by getting out of his seat and offering me his hand, leading me out of the establishment.

"You sure have a way of letting a man know what you really want, huh?" he said as we reached his Acura Integra.

I smiled back at him. "Do you have a problem with that?" I then heard the passenger door clicking open and the starting of his engine.

"I like a woman who knows what she wants," he said, chortling.

"You have great taste."

I reached over and placed my hand on his thigh and then inched it up to his crotch. His reaction was almost immediate—his member became stiff like a cucumber. Without saying a word, I leaned over, unzipped his pants and pulled his dick out of his briefs. The sight of it had my pussy creamy and soaking wet.

"Mmm, shit," he moaned as I caressed and stroked him. He then let out a gasp, sucking air once I tasted his pre-cum from the tip of my tongue.

I thought about pulling my panties to the side and stroke myself while I commenced to sucking his member. But I reminded myself that the moment and day was his. It was not long before I felt his hand on my head, nudging me to go up and down on his shaft.

Once I felt his hips thrust, I had sudden memories of Darlene McCoy, a high school classmate of mine who suffered major facial injuries while she gave head to her man after he drove into the back of a stalled car.

"Baby, why don't you find a place on the side of the road, or somewhere?" I suggested to him.

I sat up and continued caressing and stroking Kavion's dick until he pulled in behind an office building that appeared to be closed for the night. There were two other company cars in the parking lot, which was pitch dark.

"Is this better?" he asked

I leaned over and gave him a sensual kiss, sucking his tongue. He reached out and groped my breasts—he sent me into a frenzy the moment his fingers grazed over my nipples.

"Let your seat back," I instructed him.

I resumed where I left off by engulfing virtually all of his shaft down my throat without gagging—Kavion always loved that sensation. Hell, I enjoyed it so much that I hummed in tune with Adina Howard's "A Freak Like Me" blaring on the radio. I also added some loud smacking and sucking noise with my lips for added effect.

"Damn, this feels good."

"I bet it does," I responded.

"That's right. Suck this dick . . . Suck it!"

Eventually, I gave his shaft a final licking along its underside all the way up to its mushroom-shaped head, which I then sucked hard for several moments before I surprised him.

"Why'd you stop?" he queried with a look of incredulity. "I was about to bust my nut." He tried nudging me to go back down on him, but I resisted.

I prolonged his agony by guiding his engorged, dripping member back inside his pants.

"Oh I don't think so. I just wanted to give you sneak peek at what's to come. Remember, baby, good things come to those who wait."

I leaned over and kissed him on his ear lobe, licking and nibbling on it. I also fluttered my tongue inside his ear. Just as he turned to kiss me, I abruptly sat back, pulled down the passenger's make-up mirror, straightened my hair, and began reapplying some lip gloss.

Sneaking a quick glance at him, he sat there stupefied and stared hard at me. It was hard keeping a straight face. I wanted to laugh my head off, but I knew that would piss him off even more.

The mood was still light and lustful. In concession, Kavion shook his head and started his car. He sucked his teeth before he drove away.

"Girl, you know you're not right. I'm hurting over here." He rubbed his dick, closed his eyes and let out a groan like an injured animal.

"But it's a good kind of hurt." I leaned over and kissed him on the right side of his face. "I promise I'll make it worth your while when we get back to your place." I turned up the radio bobbing my head to the new beat by Donell Jones' "Where I Want to Be."

* * *

Kavion maneuvered through traffic as though he were a getaway driver. He bobbed in and out of lanes from Westwood along Sepulveda Boulevard and arrived at his apartment near the Fox Hills Mall in an astounding twenty minutes.

I mused to myself that I've always had a way with men especially when they wanted a piece of me. One look into my almond-shaped eyes, they would do practically anything I wanted.

Just ask Maxwell, my Aunt Jackie's second husband. When I was fifteen, Maxwell once came home drunk, passed out in my bed, and I woke up to him whispering and mumbling how beautiful I was. When I tried escaping, he clutched onto me tighter and refused to let go. I spent the remainder of a sleepless night with a drunk man's erection against my body.

The remainder of the week was awkward. I spent most of the time in my room. I considered telling Jackie on several occasions; however, I rationalized to myself each time that she would not believe me.

Even worse were my subsequent encounters with Maxwell.

"Cole, I-I-I'm sorry for what happened," a sober Maxwell would try appealing to me. "Please, please, don't tell your aunt. I wasn't thinking clearly. I was drunk."

Not once would I respond. I'd merely walk away, go into my room and cry.

Eventually, Maxwell went out of his way being extra nice to me. He would make my brother Marquise do the chores that I'd refuse to do. He went as far as bribing me with money. "Please, take this forty . . . I really want you to have it."

"Really, you want me to have it?"

"Yes. Just remember what happened needs to be kept between you and me—"

So I'd go to the mall and shop for clothes or just hang out with my friends with his money.

That's also when I realized if I gave a man an inch—almost literally—he'd give me whatever I wanted. I often joked that Maxwell was my first sugar daddy.

From time to time, I would catch Maxwell checking out my ass from behind especially if I bent over doing something.

"Mmm, good god!" he'd say under his breath. "Don't hurt yourself."

I'd turn around and I'd catch him jerking his hand back from having rubbed his dick through his pants. As I became more aware of my sexuality and body, I'd tease him.

"Do you really want me to hurt myself?"

"Uh-uh."

Eventually, I became bold enough to walk rather sultry towards him and place my arms around his shoulders blowing light breaths into his ear. "Then how are you going to protect me?"

"Wait until your aunt's not here."

"Okay—"

Ultimately, I gave up my virginity to Maxwell. He was such an expert with his tongue. There were times he'd beg to simply taste my pussy for a small fee or favor, of course. His tool was not bad, either, although I never experienced the pleasure of orgasms until I met Kavion.

Kavion was fast becoming a favorite pastime of mine. He stood six-two and weighed two hundred and fifteen pounds of dark chocolate, hard, lean, muscular Nubian goodness. From his pearly white teeth, to his well-defined pectoral muscles, down to his sexy ab six-pack, the sight of him during a romantic moment was more than enough to make me cream down my inner thighs.

I always thought we were an enviable couple being that he was a star football player and the fact that I more than held my own. After all, I worked out four times a week to keep my caramel legs toned and my apple bottom juicy but firm.

While I awaited him to emerge from the shower, I turned the lights down to a dimmed amber glow. I opened the blinds, allowing the moonlight to shine through. I also lit jasmine candles around the room to soften the ambience.

Next, I turned on the Bose system and loaded our favorite CDs: Classic baby making music featuring the likes of Keith Sweat, R. Kelly, D'Angelo, and Maxwell. I then made a quick scan of the room, ensuring that everything was perfect and within arm's reach. I laid the matching black-and-white fuzzy blindfold and handcuffs, warming gel, and one of my favorite accessories—a pink jackrabbit.

For dessert, I already decided on a sundae. The only thing missing from the whip cream, chocolate syrup, and strawberries was the chocolate covered banana that was connected to Kavion's body.

Once I heard him turn off the shower, I sprinted over to the mirror and gave myself a quick once-over, applying a light trail of Donna Karan perfume behind my ears and down my neck, stopping just shy of my cleavage. I also dabbed a little perfume behind my knees, and lastly along the outer edge of my manicured trim.

I glanced into the mirror, satisfied that it could not get any better. I gave myself a playful slap on the ass and pouted a berry red kiss.

When I heard the bathroom door open, I took my position— doggy style with my legs spread wide and ass pushed out—atop of his queen size bed. I was determined to hold my ground and defend my post.

"I thought you wanted to play. Aren't you going to come over here and tackle me?" I purred in my most seductive voice, looking back over my shoulder.

"You think you can handle this beat down?" he retorted, stroking himself.

I turned and sat erect, eyeing him up and down. My mouth salivated and I felt my pussy gush once I recognized his erection poking outward.

"Damn baby, that's pretty tempting. Come over here and give Butterscotch some love—"

I gestured for him to join me on the bed. He took a couple of steps before he jokingly tackled me. Playfully, I fell backwards as he landed atop me. He began kissing me from my forehead, embarking on a wet, sensual trail down to my toes. He even tantalized me by stopping to sample me from between my thighs.

"How many licks does it take to get to the creamy center?" he paused to ask.

I moaned and rocked my hips back and forth as if I were fucking his tongue. I rubbed his bald head and nudged him upward to suck my breasts. My pulsating nipples also demanded for his attention, as well. I shivered at the sensation of him gently nibbling and sucking hard on them, which was just the way I loved for my forty D's to be handled.

"Do you believe now that good things actually come to those that wait?" I bantered with him.

"Uh-huh . . ."

"Mmm, suck my pussy . . . suck my clit, baby—"

I held my legs apart for him to divulge. Immediately, I felt his tongue fluttering upon my sensitive bud. I damned near lost it the moment he began sucking it just as he did my nipples. Now I was the one sucking air and spewing expletives.

"Damn, baby. You know how to . . . oh, shit!" I said, squirming on the mattress.

I sensed by the way he shook his head that he savored every bit of nectar that I had to offer. And within moments, I felt my body tense and a torrent of orgasmic energy flow between my thighs. My breathing also quickened.

"I can't take it . . . I can't take it!"

Once I caught my breath, I held out my arms in anticipation of Kavion's long, thick chocolate dick satiating the rest of my needs.

"Fuck me, baby. Fuck me," I whispered into his ear; I also clasped my legs around his trunk, matching his long, deep strokes.

* * *

The penetration of his dick was more than worth the wait for me. Or so I thought. I felt myself on my knees hearing the sound of flesh slapping against flesh. The strokes were becoming more pronounced and deeper even as I bounced my ass hard against his body. This lasted for maybe a minute at the most before I felt him withdraw and his cum splattering on my back and ass.

Suddenly, I woke up. I still felt as if I were dreaming but the room was spinning around me and everything was a massive blur. My eyes were heavy and my body felt limp and powerless.

Next, I felt as if I were being turned onto my back and I sensed a tall, somewhat lean body lowering itself atop of me. It all seemed surreal and detached. His movements atop of me seemed deliberate and searching.

"I love you, baby. Don't worry. I'm here for you," the male figure whispered into my ear between breaths; I also began feeling the intensity of his thrusts inside of me.

At that instant, I recognized it was Barry. I thought I tried yelling and screaming for him to get off me, but it seemed as if the words never left my mouth. I tried squirming free but it seemed that Anthony and Jamil each held my arms apart in some form of a spread eagle.

Meanwhile, I tried screaming again. Nothing left my lips. I tried squirming and fighting him off of me, but I was too powerless.

"Oh, baby, you feel sooooo good. I feel it coming. Just tell me where you want it . . ."

"Get the fuck off of me!" I struggled to say.

"Oh, shit. I'm cumming. Here it is!"

I was so discombobulated that it seemed everything faded to black once again.

* * *

I woke up laying on the floor feeling disoriented. I wore only my bra and panties. My sweats were on the floor near the edge of the sofa.

In my confusion, I thought I heard a bedroom door open and a few seconds later a bathroom door open and close. Instinctively, I got up from the floor and put on my clothes. But I did not feel right. Something was wrong and I couldn't remember anything past sitting at the table playing dominoes.

I sat on the sofa trying to collect my thoughts. Flashbacks from the night before started coming to me. I recalled seeing the faces of Barry, Anthony, and Jamil.

With my face buried in my hands, Barry's voice and phrases like "I love you" and "Don't worry, I'm here for you" began invading my psyche. None of it would leave my mind. I could not help it. I had to find out.

After making myself some tea, I surveyed the apartment only to notice that Charisma and her male friend and Shanté and her male friend were still sleeping. Then it hit me again: Barry's face grimacing; Jamil's diabolical smile; Anthony's breathing behind me.

So, I ran up to my room and dialed the first phone number that came to mind.

"Hello?"

"Barry, I'm not sure. But I think something wrong happened. Do you know what happened last night?"

"What do you mean?"

"Last night, I don't remember getting undressed. I swore that I woke up to you being on top of me."

Barry was quick to respond. "Wait a minute. Whatever happened between us was consensual. I have witnesses.

This better not get back to Kendra, if you know what's good for you."

"What do you mean what's good for me, and what Kendra's gotta do with this?"

Of all people, I always maintained my distance with Barry knowing just how insecure his girlfriend Kendra, a sorority sister of mine, really was. I knew she considered me her competition, so she always kept a watchful eye on him.

"So you're telling me that you and I had sex? You've got to be kidding me. I wouldn't let you fuck me if you were the last man in Los Angeles!"

"Actually, I don't know what you're talking about. And if anything did happen, whatever happened between us would have been consensual."

He hung up the phone.

Barry's comment and threat infuriated me as I played them over and over in my mind. There was only one thing I could do. Instead of making a two-hour drive to San Diego to see my brother's competition, I decided to visit the emergency room at Daniel Freeman Hospital.

Chapter 10

Cole Kennedy
Los Angeles, California

You're going to wish you kept your mouth closed!

This was the chilling message that Barry left on my voice mail. He ranted that Kendra confronted him about our sexual encounter and broke up with him.

I stared a bit dumfounded at the phone, as if I consented to have sex with him. I closed my eyes to shut everything out and replayed those words in my mind during the drive back to my apartment.

You're going wish you kept your mouth closed!

I could take that statement in different ways, and it was not favorable for me in each scenario. There was only one option. The emergency room confirmed that something against my volition occurred, but I did not immediately press charges; it was still an option. But after that threatening phone call, I knew I needed to talk to the police.

I pulled the car into an empty parking spot near our front door, and I immediately noticed Kendra's white Honda Accord two spaces down. Damn.

First, Barry's threats, and now there was the possibility of walking into some bullshit from Kendra. I got out the car exhausted, but ready for anyone that got in my way. If Kendra was looking to start some shit with me tonight, then I was determined to get everything out in the open.

I happened to enter my apartment in the middle of Kendra's diatribe: "I should beat her high yellow ass back to Oakland where she came from . . ."

My roommates Shanté and Charisma, who were sitting around the kitchen table, chortled at her comment. The sudden door slamming shut startled them into complete silence.

Since it was obvious I was the center of their conversation, it was only natural for me to defend my reputation from lies. I gave a fake smile while I placed my purse on the stool. While I removed my jacket, I drew in slow and steady breaths; it was a struggle maintaining control. It was also a good thing I wore sweat pants and a t-shirt just in case I had to do more than just defend my name.

"Were you talking about me?" I commented, while I walked towards the refrigerator and retrieved a bottle of water.

I then turned around and leaned against the counter. I knew I had their attention because all eyes were on me. I opened the cool water bottle and took a long, satisfying drink. I made a quick assessment of my rivalry in case an altercation erupted: I was almost positive that Shanté would jump in the middle of it; I knew she would have her friend's back. I still had my reservations about Charisma. We were close, but I didn't know if her alliance with Shanté was any stronger.

"As a matter of fact, I was. " Kendra stood up from her seat rather quickly, but she happened to stay several feet from me. "Shanté told me everything. How she heard Barry sneaking out the apartment six in the morning. Just admit that you and Barry fucked!"

Kendra's voice was loud, but I was quick to realize that might be the extent of this conversation. I was not going to resort to her level. I was not going to unleash on an innocent bystander. I had a lot of pent up frustration and aggression that should be directed towards my attackers.

"Whatever you think happened did not go down like that. I don't feel like speaking on it in front of everybody, but it was not consensual; I did not willingly have sex with Barry."

"Whatever, bitch. As if I would believe Barry would force himself on you?" Kendra then snorted a dismissive laugh. "You may be cute, but I'm definitely cuter."

She copped a pose. "I don't know what games you're playing, Cole. But Barry doesn't need to force himself on anyone. I give him all the pussy he wants and needs." She looked to my roommates for support. She needed validation of her already questionable courage.

"You can believe whatever you want. I don't care, but I'm not subjecting myself with this nonsense. I know you don't want to hear about your boyfriend being accused of rape, but it did happen. Regardless of whether you believe me or not, Kendra, Barry raped me."

I was on the verge of tears, but I was not about to let them see me crack. I couldn't believe that I couldn't get an ounce of empathy from my own sorority sisters.

Kendra stepped closer. "I'm not going to allow you to dirty Barry's name. Just admit you fucked Barry because you're a slut. I am not going to stand here and let you talk about my man like that." She was so close to my face that I could taste the Doritos she ate moments ago.

Shanté confirmed my suspicion and stood aside Kendra. She spoke with just as much anger.

"Besides, I was upstairs in my bed when I heard you moaning. If you were raped it did not sound like that to me—"

There was no convincing these coconspirators of the truth. They were focused on vengeance. They only heard what they wanted. I wasn't going to waste another minute trying to persuade them to the truth—I had enough of this shit.

I dared both of them to come up on me. "I had a long day, and I'm exhausted. If anyone of you feels the need to run up on me then let's do it." I was now in my defensive stance. My fist were ready. Ready to fuck one or both of these bitches up.

Charisma spoke for the first time since I walked into this hostile situation.

"Kendra and Shanté, you need to calm down. Ya'll going to fight Cole over a man. Did you hear what she said? She was raped," she said.

"I don't need to hear that shit. Barry did not rape Cole. She's a bitch and a liar. I can't believe you would fall for this shit," Kendra yelled at Charisma.

Fuck it.

I knew if they were to gang up on me that it would not turn out good for me in the end. I headed past them towards the stairs. Again, Shanté blocked my path.

"Shanté, I don't have any beef with you. Please step aside."

I tried pushing my way past her, but she stood firm in my way. I jerked forward; Kendra pushed me from behind and I stumbled on top of Shanté. I grabbed a fistful of Shante's hair on the way down, yanking the track from her scalp. The jolt to her scalp had her screaming and kicking for me to let go, but she was at my mercy.

Charisma managed to pull Kendra off me. She kicked and punched at me, but I was determined to make Shanté bald headed. If she wanted to get in the middle of this shit, I was going to make sure she felt all the rage and frustration that had now reached a boiling point in me.

I turned my attention back to Kendra. She screamed how she was going to fuck me up.

I retorted, "What's stopping you?"

I was beyond tired of her shit. I got into her face, and I waited for her to react; she just stood there.

"Just as I thought," I said, before I walked away and headed upstairs to my room to pack a bag.

Although we had a strained relationship, I knew I could call on Sydney. Even better, she was on vacation in the Cayman Islands with a long-time friend and she allowed me to crash at her downtown condominium for a couple of weeks.

"I'm glad you're okay." Sydney said. "I'm sorry I couldn't be with you. Maybe when I return, we'll talk about what happened between you and your roommates."

It was good that I had her place all to myself. I wanted to get away from everyone I knew. Even Kavion. All I could think about is what this would do to our relationship.

"You're sure you'll be okay?" she queried once again before hanging up the phone.

"I'll be fine."

I thanked her again for the kindness. I had not given her any details. She was oblivious of the drama I was going through of late. I wasn't ready to disclose my feelings to anyone just yet. I spent the next week without any significant issues until one day after class I found three of my car tires slashed. I knew then there would be no peace. The taunts and threats from Barry and his friends infuriated me. How could I allow them to continue to get away with what they've done to me, and who knows how many other girls had fallen victim to their sick and twisted game?

A week after I reported the rape, there was a media frenzy and the story topped the headlines. That's right, three star UCLA athletes arrested for their assault against me. My only hope was that I could remain anonymous throughout this ordeal.

Chapter 11

Cole Kennedy
Los Angeles County Court
Los Angeles, California

The silence in the courtroom resonated loudly within my mind, and the tension was thicker than a third-stage smog alert. The sounds of paper shuffling from the prosecution's table to the rapid beats of my own heart paced my anticipation of this case's outcome.

I wanted badly to move on with my life after more than six months of delays, motions to dismiss, arguments, counter arguments, sidebars, and all the other drama that goes with court cases like mine.

For example during the trial, the defense tried painting me as a wild child on the loose.

Your Honor, Miss Kennedy is not without blemish. She is the product of a dysfunctional family, having seen unbridled sexual activity during her childhood years. This is the same woman who once confided in one of these three young men who possibly face incarceration that she knew that she had a gift for seduction and she knew how to prey upon one's weaknesses . . .

This is the same woman who also once confided in a mutual friend that she was, in effect, always searching for acceptance and love since it was hardly something nurtured within her family. And she befriended each of my clients for that very acceptance and love that was so much of a void in her life.

In the name of justice not only for myself, but for all, I refused to be intimidated by such nuanced, age-old bullshit used against victims of rape. "Don't let your life be dictated by these people in this courtroom," I often told myself during the trial. "You're not a bad woman. You're a strong woman who must overcome this adversity."

My attorney Sarah Dillard reminded the jury during closing arguments that the assaults on my character were unfounded, and I was nothing more than a teenager traumatized by my mother's death.

"Looking back, you realize that you cannot confide things into just anyone," I remember answering under cross-examination.

"However, my only association with Barry [Kinloch], was tutoring him with his Chemistry. Occasionally, we played dominoes. So how can one associate some aimless search for love with helping someone pass a class they were struggling in—at the request of a mutual acquaintance?"

With stellar research by Sarah and her staff, we were able to introduce as evidence that Barry, Anthony Holmes, and Jamil Holdings had similarly drugged and raped Jazzma Scott nearly two years ago on campus, and Jazzma provided testimony that we felt bolstered our argument against these three animals. The defense had none for Jazzma.

We felt confident after Sarah's final argument a little more than a day ago to the hour that this would be just a formality by the jury. But why had this taken so long?

"Mr. Foreman has the jury reached a verdict?" asked Judge Crawford Carter, whose voice caused me to shudder and grab Kavion's hand.

"Yes we have, Your Honor," the foreman responded; chest deflated upon completing his response. He appeared as if he was the most important person in the world—at this moment he was at least in mine. My mouth went dry and my stomach tightened. I squeezed Kavion's hand even tighter. He squeezed back, assuring me that everything was all right.

Carter, an older but burlier version of Hugh Jackman, reached for the folded slip of white paper that was handed to him by the bailiff. He opened the slip and closed it, remaining stoic before a courtroom gathering that seemed now to hang on every movement and nuance.

"Will the defendants rise—"

Anthony, Barry, and Jamil all looked at each other and then sprung to their feet looking straight ahead. On this particular day, their appearance bore little resemblance of that fateful night in my apartment when they were drunk and forceful. They were monsters and deceptive thieves that stole a part of my heart, spirit, and soul.

Now, they had freshly-cropped haircuts and were dressed sharply in dark-colored suits. Their faces were of contrition and concern.

After all, they were being tried for first-degree rape and we pushed for the maximum sentencing of eight years, according to the state's penal code.

"Your Honor, on the charges of first-degree rape, we, the jury, find Anthony Holmes not guilty," the foreman announced.

NOT GUILTY?

I could not believe what I heard. Immediately, my mind went into a semi-daze and my ears rung; the foreman continued with the reading of the verdicts.

"For Barry Kinloch, the jury also finds him not guilty of first-degree rape . . . and Jamil Holdings, the jury finds him not guilty of first-degree rape."

The courtroom was a mixture of celebration and pandemonium. Anthony, Barry, and Jamil reacted by pumping their fists and hugging their attorneys. Their respective family members erupted into shouts of praising and thanking God. Conversely, there were shrieks of disbelief and loud rumblings behind me. I could not control the tears that streamed down my face as thoughts of humiliation, ridicule, and horror bombarded me. Now I understood why some people react in the courtroom the way they do when a gross injustice has occurred...

"How could I not be vindicated by this horrendous crime?" I cried, looking over at Kavion. "The system was hoodwinked by money and fame."

"Baby, I'm sorry," he whispered back to me.

"Sorry for what?" I reacted. "I never thought a jury would believe that I wanted those animals to force themselves upon me or believe that I was willing to take a date-rape drug."

"Baby, I—"

My vision was now blurred and my eyes stung from the tears. The sound of Judge Carter's gavel was like gunshots to my soul while he shouted, "Order in the Court . . . Order in the Court!"

What fucking order? I fumed.

Judge Carter looked to his left and nodded. "Thank you, Mr. Foreman. You are free to go." And he looked in the direction of the three that violated me. "Young men, you are free to go."

Surely, they were free to go on with their lives as though nothing had ever happened to me or Jazzma. Sarah tried advising me on the rights I had filing an appeal. But none of that registered with me. I felt reduced to leaving the courtroom feeling even more of a prisoner of the system.

Chapter 12

Stefan Lewis
Los Angeles, California

I collapsed onto the hotel queen-sized bed drained and tired from the long drive from Seattle. I did not bother to take off my jacket or shoes. I picked up the remote control that was lying on the night stand near the bed and turned on the television.

The very first image that I saw captivated me. She was butter pecan complexioned with sandy brown hair, and her eyes were almond shape—the color of amber leaves on a fall morning. She wore a two-piece grey wool suit. Although ostensibly distraught, she remained demure and coherent as she spoke to the horde of media hounds with their microphones aimed at her.

I perked up instantly, but I needed a closer look. So, I scooted to the edge of the bed and sat closer to the nineteen-inch color television. The reception, however, was not as clear.

Ugh!

I slapped the side of the TV hoping the reception would improve—I knew I should have spent more instead of saving a few bucks at this Super 8 hellhole just off Prairie Avenue.

"Ms. Kennedy, Ms. Kennedy . . . do you have any comment about the jury's verdict?" a female reporter shouted.

Next to her stood a rather tall, handsome dark-skinned man who tried shielding her from the reporters converging closer.

"How would you think any victim of a crime would feel in a situation as this?" She responded. "You put your faith in the system hoping for justice because it is supposed to prevail. But sometimes it is flawed, and now you're among the thousands of victims not believed . . ."

I watched intensely while she interacted. My heart began to ache severely for her. There was something about the passion in her eyes that spoke to my soul.

"I am devastated that these crimes were not vindicated. Words cannot express the sadness that fills my heart now." Her eyes began welling tears, one even escaped down from her eye slit; her upper lip quivered.

Immediately, I felt a kindred connection to her. How could that jury acquit them of the charges that were brought before them?

The man next to her nudged her to continue walking. As they forced their way, she continued, "This trial has been nothing short of a heart-wrenching ordeal. There will come a day when these monsters will have to face their Maker and beg for their own forgiveness." She placed a hand over her mouth. The man next to her placed his arm around her and stiff-armed a cameraman. He escorted her to a black sedan.

The horde's attention had now turned to some well-dressed man, quite possibly wearing an Italian wool suit, who was also walking away from the court building. He seemed to savor the opportunity to address them.

"Mr. Black, may we get a moment?" a reporter asked. "Did you ever think there was ever any doubt with the jury's verdict?"

It was apparent that Mr. Black was an attorney. There were three athletic-looking young men that stood behind him. And behind the three were a smattering of people who were visibly elated, nodding their heads. I was more than curious as to what these bastards had to say.

"My clients can now go on with their lives without the ordeal and stigma of rape looming over their heads," he said. "We do sincerely hope that Ms. Kennedy and Ms. Scott can get the help they need.

"However way you want to put it, the system is fair. This case was tried by a jury of their peers and they believed there was no wrongdoing by my clients . . . I ask that you respect these young men and their respective family's privacy. Thank you."

The outright arrogance of this bastard, I hissed and shook my head in disbelief.

Just as they began walking from the courthouse, the same female reporter pursued them. "Barry Kinloch, can you comment on anything regarding a mystery tape of the rape? I've heard that several people have seen it."

The cameraman went past the reporter and focused his lens on the young man. He captured her aiming a microphone just behind him. The jovial look on his face turned into furrowed eyebrows. But someone from his contingent walked up to the cameraman and placed his hand over the lens. The station cut back to the studio and then went to a commercial break.

Long after what I witnessed on television, I still found myself staring absently at the tube thinking and wondering how Ms. Kennedy lived. Just the thought of her had given me a second wind of energy.

She reminded me of my former fiancée Fiona, whom I dearly missed, from the way she had her hair pulled back in a tight chiffon bun, drawing the focus on her high cheek bones and soft features. It made her look regal, rather queenly in fact.

I stood up and studied myself in the mirror. My mother had always said I had eyes of a charmer. She was right. I could charm the panties off a nun. And before LaSalle ruined everything for me, I had many girls begging to give me head all because they loved the color of my dreamy eyes and chiseled good looks. That's right. I had conquered plenty of pussy because I looked so much like a movie star.

Although I've now turned twenty-eight and gained a little weight, I still feel I've had what it takes. Many times, I've heard that I resemble Rick Fox the actor, former basketball player and ex to Vanessa Williams. And just think, he had the best of both worlds.

I ran my hand through my hair. It's just as wavy as Fox's. But, wow, my hairline's showing signs of receding just like him. Maybe it's genetics. Maybe it's been the stress of what I'd gone through back in Seattle. I could certainly go for a much easier lifestyle. That's the reason why I'm here in Los Angeles.

Tomorrow, I've got an interview scheduled at one o'clock for a pharmaceutical sales representative gig. Not bad for somebody who graduated in the top ten percent of his class.

Chapter 13

Cole Kennedy
Los Angeles, California

The ensuing months following the verdict proved to be most difficult. There was no normalcy in my life.

I did what many women who were raped have done—I tried to avoid it. If I did not talk about it, then it did not exist. Unfortunately, it did happen, and I was often reminded of the rape and its outcome seemingly at every turn.

I was threatened with physical violence for "lying" on a star athlete. Usually, that occurs prior to, during, or immediately after the rape. But I was confronted one afternoon by three women in the parking lot of a Ralph's supermarket in Santa Monica.

"I saw you on TV," one of them said; she stood about five-six, a couple of inches shorter than me. "I really felt sorry for you."

The fact she said she felt sorry for me caused me to be less suspicious.

"Yeah, she might have felt sorry for you. But she really doesn't, bitch," a taller somewhat masculine-type woman hissed. "Who in the fuck do you think you were trying to accuse my cousin of rape?

"I ought to fuck your ass up right here, right now, in broad fucking daylight."

I was stupefied. The words never left my mouth in forming a response. I started walking away from them, hoping like hell that someone saw what was happening. I did not even bother to recall what the third woman look like, but her voice was just as threatening as the other two.

"That's right. Take your ass on, you fucking whore. Because that's what you are!" she yelled at me. I hurried back inside the store and I waited about a half-hour before I tried going back out to the parking lot.

After that encounter, I withdrew from everyone I used to associate with and lived my life as a recluse. The ordeal had taken something from me and I wanted it back. I just wished I knew what it was. I needed closure to figure out this mess I called my life. I was tired of the lack of sincerity from people who once called themselves friends and acquaintances of mine, the taunting, and their teasing. I thought about leaving school, but I refused to let anything affect my goal of graduating.

Making matters worse, although I knew it would take time for the wounds to heal, I did not expect that my relationship with Kavion would suffer the most. I grew tired of his accusations and distrust.

Trust, as I had come to learn, was something that when it's lost is forever gone.

"Cole, you don't know what it feels like when everyone you know is laughing behind your back," he confided in me during a phone conversation. "Or having to hear rumors that your girl was fucking around with athletes, and then within a couple of weeks had wild sex with three of my friends."

"Really Kavion? Are you fucking serious? I was raped!" I retorted. "That's why I know we can't be together any longer."

With deep resignation, I went on to say, "Kavion, I know this ordeal has been difficult for you losing a few friends and defending me in the process." I recalled pausing, in wonderment, as much as the thought of losing him. The thought of losing him hurt; however, I did not want to lose myself even more in the process.

"If it means anything to you, I want you to know that I was always faithful to you. But I can't continue living my life this way. I will not allow myself to go through another interrogation or another prosecution from you or anyone else. I did not ask for this, but I also know you did not, either."

"You know what? Maybe we do need to go our separate ways. I just can't deal with the stigmas anymore."

"Kavion, you don't know what you're saying—"

"Oh, yes I do, Cole."

Exhaling deeply, I offered, "Kavion, you're right. You don't trust me. I can't make you trust me if you don't want to trust and believe me."

I proceeded to hang up on him.

The break up with Kavion sent me into depression. I had not been that way since my mother's death nor had I felt so much alone.

Amidst all the drama and emotional turmoil, I started receiving bouquets of flowers with notes stating that I was not alone. Initially, I thought they came from Kavion.

"Since when did you become a flower-sending man?" I asked him.

"What are you talking about?" Kavion responded, dryly. "I haven't sent you anything."

"Well, the reason why I'm calling you is that I've been receiving bouquets of flowers lately. And I thought since you and I had that disagreement that maybe—"

"I guess you're not wasting any time getting yourself back on the market," Kavion retorted.

His snide remarks did not resonate well with me nor did it require a response other than me slamming the phone in his ear once again.

Life went on. Having an admirer made the difficult times easier knowing someone out there was looking out for me. I just wish I knew who it was so I could thank him or her. I started receiving flowers at work like clockwork every Monday right before lunch. Then I started receiving them on Friday's right before leaving my internship at Brinkley and Stewart law firm in Los Angeles.

* * *

One Friday evening after work, I arrived home and was met by two detectives sitting in the lobby. The one closest to me appeared to be in his forties, the years of witnessing death showed through his eyes and face. I was cowed by his appearance. His eyes were hard and hollow and the dark circles underneath made him gauntly.

"Hello. Ms. Kennedy?" He rose out of his seat to greet me. I was scared to touch his bony jaundiced hand.

"Yes, and you are?" I asked as I extending my right hand.

"I'm Detective Jenkins. Steve Jenkins." He looked to his right. "And this is my partner, Detective Ramirez."

Ramirez nodded and extended his hand. He stayed in the background.

"I'm afraid we have a bit of bad news," Jenkins said. "Do you mind if we continue this conversation in your apartment?"

The tone in his voice was more of a demand than a request. Although I wanted to duck and hide, I agreed and I invited them upstairs into my apartment. The elevator ride to the fifth floor was the longest forty-five seconds of my life. All kinds of shit raced through my mind. The small talk did nothing for my nerves. A year and a half later, I knew this day would come. I thought the incident with The Cyclone was coming to light. I wished that I had enough courage back then to say something. I would have come out looking like a hero rather than a murderer.

When we entered my apartment, I invited them to a seat on my cream suave sectional sofa. I offered them something to drink but they both declined. Which was fine by me, I wanted to get straight to the reason why they were here.

"You mentioned there was bad news, is my family okay?"

Detective Jenkins replied, "No. I'm sorry I should have elaborated in the lobby; we are here to investigate the death of Barry Kinloch. We understand your relationship took a sour turn after you accused him of rape."

I dismissed his statement. Actually, I did not really hear anything pass Barry being dead.

"Barry's dead?" I paused slightly. "I did not know . . . Oh, I see. You think I had something to do with it." The purpose of the visit became quite evident. I was a suspect in a murder. Maybe the only suspect.

"You don't honestly believe I had anything to do with it? Do I need to call an attorney, detectives?" I asked while searching for my cell phone that was buried beneath a shit load of junk in my purse.

"Only if you have something to hide, Ms. Kennedy?" divulged Detective Ramirez, who spoke for the first time since our introductions. His voice was soothing. He should speak more often, I noted to myself, although I did not particularly appreciate his insinuation.

"I don't have anything to hide, detectives. Considering our past, I'm not saying that I'm sorry he's dead, but I had nothing to do with his death. So how did he die?" My question was directed more to Ramirez than Jenkins. His face was softer and nicer looking.

"It was a hit-and-run. The eyewitnesses reported seeing a light-colored car leaving the scene. If you don't mind, could you please tell us where you were last night between the hours of eight and eleven?"

I was not threatened by his questioning, I knew it was routine, especially considering Barry and I had a bad history.

"I was home by seven, and I stayed here all night."

He asked if anyone could corroborate my story. I informed him that I was home alone working on my thesis.

"I forgot. I had Chinese delivered and that was at 8:45 p.m.," I continued. "Other than that, I guess I don't have much of an alibi. But, whatever you need to do, I will not stand in your way."

I stood to signal I was ending the conversation. Both officers stood up; Detective Ramirez pulled a card from his suit pocket.

"Ms. Kennedy, if you have any additional information please call me at the number listed on the card." He bowed his head slightly and proceeded towards the front door.

Detective Jenkins' dark eyes burned a hole through my skull; I could not wait for him to leave. He made my skin feel dirty and the first thing I was dying to do was take a shower.

Just as Detective Jenkins crossed the threshold, he turned around reminiscent of a classic Peter Falk moment from the Colombo series. The only thing missing was him having a stogie in his hand.

"May I ask what color is your car?"

"I have a gold Lexus."

He started grinning, as if he'd caught me in a lie. "Do you mind letting us inspect your vehicle for damages?

"My car is in the garage, and you're welcome to check for any damages," I answered, motioning with my head and hand in that direction. Besides, I knew there would be none. "Would you need my keys for further inspection?"

"We'll call if we have any other questions. Good night, Ms. Kennedy," Jenkins answered.

After they left, I plopped on the couch. I figured whatever karma had in store for Barry was brought on by his actions. But, I still could not believe he was dead. I hated him for what he did to me but I could never wish death on a person. Especially when I knew he may have never repented for his sins.

I needed a friend, but that list was practically non-existent. I did not know whom I could call. I had not spoken to Sydney in a few weeks and Kavion even longer. I ended up contacting Marquise, who was still on his tour of duty in Sierra Leone. Even so, I could only do that by letter.

Chapter 14

Sydney Starks
Los Angeles, California

Caramella Girl had become almost everything that I had dreamt it would become. My girls were in constant demand by their clientele, and the money kept rolling in. And unlike the examples from my mother's past, I had done well with my money.

Although I had not brought it up with my business partner Reggie, I began thinking that it was time for Caramella Girl to expand from a local operation to something regional, bordering national.

All it would take was the right connections—and they were fast coming together. That's right, there was more than one way to becoming rich.

Mmm, there goes one of my sources of independent wealth contacting me . . .

"Caramella Girl?"

"Yes, I would like to make arrangements for a meeting tomorrow evening," the caller said. "Is that something that can be arranged?"

"I'm sorry, but we do not facilitate that quick of a turnaround. We would like to make sure that our escorts are in the safest of environments. Would you hold please?"

"Sure, okay. I guess—"

I had learned early on never to accept just any offer. Besides, my business was based on referrals other than direct contact in which I've personally met a potential client.

"May I ask who referred you to Caramella Girl?"

"Certainly, a very prominent county judge. I don't like mentioning his name. I think you can understand."

"I do respect the privacy of my clients, but this is also business," I responded, having become suspicious of how in the hell he had my number in the first place.

He sighed into the phone.

"I would really not want to divulge his name. Do you have any other questions?"

"Listen here, I don't know how you obtained my number, but if I were you I'd make a very short fucking memory of it."

Click!

Silly motherfucker.

That's just proof why I may need to expand my business and perhaps find somebody whom I could trust to filter out our clients. That would be one less stressful thing I would have to concern myself with.

For all I know, that may have been a private investigator who was hired by a scorned wife. Those bastards really think they can fool somebody. And if it was, that was her fucking problem, not mine. I hope if there was any sex involved with him she liked the taste of my girls' pussy—double if it were mine.

Today really must be my day. I've loved the fact that Caramella Girl's in demand, but come on. There are times when I would prefer to have a day just to myself, which I can. But how many jobs are there out there where a woman can mix business and pleasure and get fucking paid for it?

At least this call is a friendly one. I easily recognized the number. I met this son of a Japanese banking magnate at a party I attended with another client in Beverly Hills, and he's been after me ever since.

"Why hello, Akeno. What honor have I deserved for you to call me?"

His dialect was very pronounced and his laugh was very hearty. But for all the mumbo-jumbo bullshit, the man actually had a brain. It actually intrigued me.

"Ah, yes. I still can't get over that I saw someone as beautiful as you. A man might have opportunities like meeting you once, maybe twice in his life," he said. "It is more of an honor that you would allow me to call you."

"Why thank you."

I had to remind myself about business. This shit's never personal.

"Akeno, may I ask why are you calling me today?"

"Yes, I've been thinking about you since the first time we've met—"

"You've already told me that."

"Sure. I have a business partner who is coming in from New York soon, and I want to show him a good time. I would like for you to accompany me, and, uh . . ."

"You would like somebody to accompany him?"

"Yes. That is right."

"You do know that this is strictly business. You do know that I require certain level of reimbursement."

He laughed at my comment. "Money is not an object with me. Men of my background lavish women with great gifts."

"I'm glad you understand that. If I do agree to this, I will require at least three thousand; it may be more if things reach another level—"

"That is not a problem. But what about my friend coming in from New York? I would like somebody who is very intelligent and professional in her demeanor."

I did not immediately respond to Akeno's comment. Actually, I had to think about it. While none of my women were cheap hussies, I was not aware of any who were known for their intellect and having actual goals in life.

"I think I have somebody who would complement your 'friend' very well. Of course, that will be extra," I finally told him.

"I would like for you and your associate to set aside next Friday for accompanying me and my friend," he said. "You have my number. I will make sure that my transaction is conducted as smoothly as possible."

There was nothing more of a turn-on than a man who had his shit together.

"Very good. I will contact you in a couple of days. I will have more on the person who will accompany your friend at that time."

"Thank you."

The only person that came to mind was Cole. But I had not spoken to her since she spent a couple of weeks in my place while I was out of town. I liked the fact she kept my place clean, and she appeared to have replaced what she ate from my refrigerator.

For the longest, I had offered her a chance to make some extra money by doing work for me, but I never pushed the issue since we've been friends—or something like that.

The best thing that she had done was keeping her mouth shut about The Cyclone. She was just as much to blame for his death, OD'ing on that fucking cocaine.

I may be going against my better judgment, but it may be worth the while. Besides, if she doesn't accept, I know three or four others who would accept without asking any questions.

Taking a deep breath, I willed myself into dialing her number. Humph, I was surprised that she answered but she sounded so listless.

"Cole, what's the matter with you?" I asked, forgetting that it had been several months since we've last spoken.

"Is this Sydney?"

"Girl, don't play silly with me."

"I'm not. I, uh, just haven't been the socializing type lately. I've pretty much done what I've had to do, and just stay to myself."

"Well, it's time that you come out of your cave, or from under that rock."

"What are you talking about?" she retorted. "In case, you haven't heard since you've traveled the world in search of the next trick to turn, I was denied justice and I've had people to turn their backs on me."

"In case you forgot, I was there for you the last time you called me. Maybe you've forgotten about people who know you." I refused to be caught up on any guilt game, and my patience was wearing thin.

"Cole," I tried reasoning with her, "I called you because I was thinking about you. Yeah, maybe we haven't talked or seen each other in a while. But I'm still here. Sometimes, you've got to make the effort to reach out to other people."

I paused and allowed those words to settle in with her. The fact she had not talked shit back to me suggested that they may have hit the right place.

"I don't know what happened. Maybe I was out of town, or maybe out of the country. I'm sorry if what you're telling me did happen—"

"Yes it did," she reacted. "I thought that those three animals that drugged and raped me would be behind bars having to fight off other prisoners who literally would want a piece of their asses. But they're out there on the streets, free as a fucking jaybird."

"No, I didn't hear about that. But you've got to move on. You can't stay to yourself forever," I said. "Maybe it is good that I am calling you."

"And why is that?"

I knew that this was not the time to talk business with Cole, but there are ways of getting what I want.

"It doesn't matter. We're friends. We've known each other since college. It's time that you come out of your shell.

There's a big, fucking world out there, girl, and you need to see it."

"That can wait. My energy has been on finishing college. I don't have much longer to go."

"I'm not saying you shouldn't finish college. But if you've not been mixing among other people, then maybe you need to take a little time away."

"I'm not interested."

"You're not interested in seeing me?" I said. "I ought to come over there and beat your ass."

Cole began laughing. At least that was a good sign. "You know what? You're right. I'm glad that you called me."

Chapter 15

Stefan Lewis
Los Angeles, California

I noticed him entering Fisher's Cove, which appeared to be a popular bar not far from Washington Boulevard in the Marina Del Rey section of town. Just inside the place, I also noticed a woman, who was rather tall but slightly on the thin side, approach him and give him a hug. His hands slid down from her shoulders, resting at the small of her back.

This was not surprising about Anthony Holmes. After all, I had spent the past five weeks studying him as if I were an actor learning a new character and script. I knew that after each UCLA home basketball game that he liked going there.

Humph. Such arrogance. Another privileged motherfucker who had the world at his beckoning and women seemingly throwing themselves at him simply because he could dribble a basketball and shoot it better than ninety-nine, point nine-nine percent of the rest of the world.

Whereas, I toiled four and a half years for the education that I earned without any attention from fans, groupies, or the media. People like me would still have a say in how much money he might make down the road.

So, I finished my cigarette before I left my car, a Ford Thunderbird—the only thing that I liked about it was the eight-cylinder engine. I also made sure that my fake mustache and wig piece were in place.

When I entered the crowded establishment, I spotted Anthony and his company in the back playing pool. The site of him and that woman evoked bad memories in my own life. But neither he nor she would be an issue much longer. Not at all. Nor was I going to back out now. I was determined that everything would go according to plan.

I ordered a soda for myself and glanced at the television. There was something about UCLA's victory over a ranked opponent and just my luck, there were highlights of him making the winning basket.

"Would you like anything else?" the bartender interrupted my train of thought; I surprised myself that I did not shudder upon hearing his burly voice.

"Yeah, sure. Give me a bottle of Heineken, thank you."

"Sure, coming right up."

The beer was definitely cold, a good thing about visiting places like this. I headed over to the pool table where he was playing with the woman. I waited until it was his turn before I approached him.

"Anthony," I yelled. "That was a hell of a game you played. Ten seconds on the clock, you're down by a point and you take the ball from half court . . ."

I mimicked his shooting motion before continuing, "Pump fake and then swoosh! Game over and you win."

He straightened up from the table and smiled. He was a bit taller than I had imagined. "So I take it that you were at the game, huh?"

I knew that I had his attention at least for the moment. "Yeah, right over there." I smiled and nodded over at the television.

"Yeah, right." He leaned forward over the pool table and took aim. For someone who had skills on a basketball court, they also seemed to translate well with a pool cue in his hand. He made an impressive bank shot, pocketing the six-ball in the far corner.

"You're on a roll there." I stopped and focused my attention on the lady. "I'm sorry. Please excuse my excitement and ignorance. My name is Kyle." I held my hand out to her.

"I'm Natasha." Although a bit uncomfortable, she was cordial and accepted my shaking her hand.

I then turned my attention back to him. "Anthony, I'm Kyle." I held out my fist to give him a fist bump. "I don't want to interrupt what you two are doing, but may I buy the two of you something?"

He looked over at her, then back at me. "Sure, why not?"

"Would a beer be all right for both of you?"

"I usually don't drink any during the season. But since you're buying, I'll have a shot of some cognac—Remy—and she'll have a strawberry daiquiri." He paused and looked at me. "That's if you're serious about getting me one."

I reached into my pocket and flashed my short stack of money. "Does that look like I'm serious? Your shot made me two thousand tonight."

"I guess that means you are buying."

"I'll be right back."

It still took a lot not to bull rush him and beat his ass with one of the cue sticks for what he had done to Cole. In my infiltrating the student population to learn more about Anthony, I found out that he had openly bragged of being the one who either held her legs or arms apart while his other two friends raped her.

On his part, he did not penetrate her but he fucked her breasts—only because he felt he should have been first. That dubious distinction went to Barry and to his credit, or detriment, he recently had a meeting with destiny.

"All right, daiquiri for you, Natasha . . . and a shot of Remy for you," I said upon my return. I also mused at how young and somewhat gullible he was. He failed to recognize that this was not like a party on campus.

"You're okay, man," Anthony said. "Thanks."

Just as I was about to challenge him to a game, I overheard in the background a group of people also calling for UCLA's star basketball player.

"Yo, Anthony. What up?" one said.

"Yeah, nigga. You a bad motherfucker!" another said, adding a basketball player's shooting motion to his comment.

"I told y'all about making a scene," Anthony said.

I turned around and noticed two guys in their early twenties grinning as they approached him. Both were dressed as if they were two-bit playas wearing gold in their mouths and what seemed to be everywhere else possible on them. It was also clearly evident that I was soon to be the odd man out. Literally.

So, I was quick to come up with another angle of attack: I walked off and went over to the bar, glanced occasionally at television, and observed them as well. After watching them shoot the shit for another twenty minutes or so, I made another pass by their playing table.

"Yo, fella. You gonna hook up my partners like you did me and my lady friend here?"

I chortled. "That was a personal gift from me to you."

"I see."

I noticed that he still had some of his cognac remaining. His lady friend had already finished her daiquiri. "Since I'm such a good guy, I'll get one more for you and another for your lady friend. Your friends will have to help themselves."

He shrugged his shoulders and continued playing while Natasha seemed to have resigned herself to being just a trophy piece on this particular night.

"Okay, you do that."

When I returned with their drinks this time, I had already "sprinkled" his with a concoction similar to what he and those animals had given Cole.

Now it was time to watch . . . and wait. In a matter of minutes, Anthony's speech was slurred and he weaved while he stood. It was so amusing to see the sudden change just as it was that nobody had yet to suspect anything mischievous on my part.

"Say, baby. You down for sucking my dick right here?" Anthony inquired of Natasha. I was not surprised that he'd say something like that knowing during my surveillance of him that it was a common thing for women to oblige him at parties—and in some cases while he was out on the dance floor.

She promptly replied, "Not here. Too many people around." Then she sucked her teeth. "But it's something I wouldn't mind doing."

"What do you mean? It's just me, you, my partners, and, uh, what's his face. You know, homebody who gave us these drinks," he responded. "I don't think they'd have a problem with you doing it right here."

I had long since taken a seat not far from their pool table and continued watching and waiting.

"Damn, playa. You trying to get a hook-up in here?" one of his friends said.

"Why not?" Anthony countered.

"You know what? I don't think you can handle your liquor."

"Shut up, motherfucker. I can handle my shit, your shit, and any other motherfucker's in this damn place."

Despite his thug looks, the other friend was more of a voice of reasoning. "Looks like to me you getting fucked up. Last thing you need is to get in trouble."

Anthony looked at them and his lady friend. "Yeah, think I better take my ass on. I'm outta here. You coming with me?"

Perhaps it was the wisest thing to do. After all, it had also been mentioned that he was regarded as a high draft pick, and that meant he was soon to make millions playing professionally.

The party that had so much potential quickly dispersed. Anthony's two other friends had given their hugs and fist-bumps. That was also my cue to navigate my way through the crowd in anticipation of Anthony's departure.

From my vantage point, I saw Anthony walk rather carefully out to his Mazda in the parking lot. Natasha appeared to have tried talking to him, but his arm movements among other things may have suggested that he felt capable of driving.

I observed him pulling out of the driveway and zipping out into traffic as if he were a NASCAR driver. I found it challenging to follow him because he weaved in and out of traffic and cars blared their horns at him. It was a miracle that there was no police in the area or they might have stopped him for driving under the influence.

Now that would be funny, I thought.

Somehow, Anthony made his way onto the Santa Monica Freeway. I had no clue as to why he took that route. Maybe he needed to clear his head or something.

He drove about a mile before he decided to exit. He appeared to continue driving at a fast rate of speed. Then I saw his brake lights, and his car entered into a hard skid. His tires screeched loudly. It was apparent that he tried to avoid hitting a car that had stopped suddenly before him. It happened so fast, but I saw his car plow over a traffic sign situated on a lane median used at off-ramps.

Then it was ka-boom!

His car crashed violently into a light post, wrapping itself around it.

I could not believe what had transpired before me. I slowed down to capture a glimpse: There was a large dent on driver's side of the vehicle and both the driver and passenger side windows were blown out. There was smoke coming from the engine. I saw a body slumped over.

Nobody had bothered to stop and see if there was anything wrong with him. Humph. Nor was I.

Early the next morning, I saw on the news that UCLA basketball star Anthony Holmes, twenty years old, had died in a traffic accident. I didn't think there was any chance of survival, but I knew that justice had been duly served.

There was a shot from the crash scene with flowers around the light post. That segued into people at UCLA visibly distraught, some even crying inconsolably, as they tried to make sense of what happened to him.

"This is terrible. Absolutely terrible," an athletic department official commented. "I'm shocked, grief stricken . . . Just last night, Anthony had one of the most electrifying performances I'd ever seen . . . And about three o'clock this morning, I get a call that he's gone . . ."

I was pissed that there was no mentioning of him being named a defendant in Cole's case. That just goes to show how privileged motherfuckers like him are even in death.

Perhaps Cole will express some gratitude that somebody like myself truly cares for her because that's exactly what she needs right now in her life.

Chapter 16

Cole Kennedy
Los Angeles, California

First, Barry was found dead. He was the victim of a hit-and-run. Now I've just heard that Anthony died in a car accident. It was said that he was driving intoxicated on alcohol and some other drugs that were in his system; they were still waiting on the toxicology report. The fact that two of my attackers were dead within a matter of weeks had me freaking out. I could hardly sleep.

Just my luck, the police showed up again at my place during one of the busiest weeks of the school year. I had a thesis paper that I was close to completing; it accounted for nearly half of my grade this semester.

"Ms. Kennedy, I'm sorry to bother you again," Detective Stevens greeted me at the door; he looked in back of him. "And you do remember Detective—"

"Yes, I do. Detective Ramirez," I answered.

"We wanted to inform you that our investigation into Barry Kinloch's death is still ongoing. We've not ruled out anything as of yet."

"Is that right?"

"That is correct."

"Then might I ask why you're here?"

Detective Stevens entered into a pause. He took a deep breath before he continued. "We came here because we have a few more questions."

I still had not allowed them to come inside my place. In fact, it was becoming more difficult to hide my annoyance. "I was questioned after those animals raped me. I was questioned when I sought justice. Now I'm being questioned again because one of them didn't know how to look both ways before he crossed the damn street."

Stevens reached into his pocket for his notepad. "I wish it was as easy as you just surmised." He looked up at me. Once again, I felt as though his dark eyes burned a hollow hole into my soul. I knew that I would have to take a shower as soon as he and his partner left.

"You are not a suspect. However, we still have questions to ask you."

"And what might they be?" I hissed.

"Did you have any contact with Mr. Kinloch after your trial?"

"No."

"And you were never romantically involved with him—at any time ever?"

"God no!"

"How would you characterize the extent of your acquaintance with him?"

"It was an acquaintance at best." I shook my head in disgust. "Look, why don't you get the transcript of the trial. I answered similar questions like this—under oath."

"I understand your being uncomfortable. This is not double-jeopardy."

"Then why are you here?" I responded. "Clearly, you're trying to establish some motive. But I have none. I've tried as best as I can to go on with my life. "

"Ms. Kennedy—"

"If I am going to be interrogated every time someone dies in this city," I snapped, cutting off Detective Ramirez before he could continue, "then I think I need to speak with my lawyer. I will not be intimidated by your tactics. So if you don't mind, I have a paper to finish. Good day." I slammed the door in their faces and I returned to my thesis.

God, why is this happening to me?

They've definitely ruined my thinking; I guess my thesis would have to wait. I turned off my computer and retired for the day.

I called Kavion, although we were not talking. It was just the fact that he was a great listener was one of things I missed about him.

"Kavion?"

"Is this who I think it is?"

"Yes, it's me, Cole." His voice was more than a welcomed thing to me. It allowed me to unwind and be myself for the first time in quite a while.

"And what has earned me this honor?"

"To be honest, I just need someone that I could talk to. It's been a struggle since the trial."

"It's got to be tough on you. But you're strong. Your strength was something I always admired about you," he said.

I then shared with him about my being questioned by the police twice as it pertained to Barry's death. "They're trying to build a case with me as a suspect. All circumstantial. They've not ruled it a murder or anything else. But I know they've got to start somewhere; it isn't with me."

"How did he die?" There was a bit of surprise and intrigue in his voice.

"He got hit by vehicle. Guess he didn't look both ways."

"For real?"

"I don't know if that was how it happened. But he is dead," I answered. "And if that's not enough, I saw on the news that Anthony's also dead. Car accident."

Then it occurred to me that Anthony and Kavion were good friends.

"Oh, I forgot. How are you doing, Are you going to the funeral?"

"I don't know about us being friends. One of the last times we spoke, we argued about you."

"About me? What about?" I thought I already knew why, but I just needed to hear it from him.

He divulged that he confronted Anthony about the alleged video tape of the rape. "He didn't deny you were raped, but that he did not have sex with you." I sensed the anger in his voice. "I wanted to kill him. I lunged at him but a couple of other frat brothers pulled me off him. I've not spoke to him since."

I had not heard any stories like that. Then again, I had not associated myself with anyone since breaking up with Kavion. But just the thought of him confronting Anthony perked me up a notch.

"Why didn't you call me?" I queried. "It would have been nice to know someone believed me."

Sighing, Kavion told me that he wanted to call me so many times. "I had the phone in my hands but I punked out."

I already recognized why he had not called: Pride.

"I made such of fool of myself I did not know what to say to you."

"Sorry could have worked—"

"You're right. I apologize, Cole. For everything."

Although this could have helped in my healing process, maybe breaking up would have never happened. Regardless, that conversation was therapeutic. I needed to know I wasn't alone and that I had people, if not friends, in my corner. I needed to know that the light was near.

Chapter 17

Stefan Lewis
Los Angeles, California

Two motherfuckers down, one more to go. I made the honorable decision to take care of what the law and a jury refused to do.

The decision wasn't hard once I also found out that they raped a few other young women — all but one of them were too afraid to come forward. They don't have to be anymore. They can now go on and live their lives without an ominous cloud over their heads.

More importantly, nobody's going to brag and boast about how he hurt Ms. Cole Kennedy, the love of my life, and live to talk about it. Nobody. I'll vindicate her honor every time.

Apparently, Barry Kinloch did not think I would. He went around telling individuals that Ms. Kennedy challenged to take on him and his friends at her apartment. "I can put [porn star] Jada Fire to shame with my moves."

To which Barry bragged, "She told me to make sure that we had it on video . . . She kept saying that her titties were just as big as Jada's and her ass is much juicier."

What Barry did not understand was how I would go as far as robbing Peter to pay Paul — I tricked a Mexican into giving me a ride only to rob him of his car—in order to silence his ass for making those uncouth statements.

Talk about deer in the headlights? It was more like Barry in the headlights.

Need I say anymore?

And that brings me to another point. I also learned that the guy who accompanied Ms. Kennedy from the courthouse was her ex-boyfriend. I can't explain how much of an honor I've considered it being in her life knowing, too, that she went as far as dumping her ex, Kavion Cottrell, in favor of me.

Apparently, she recognized that he never had the capacity to protect her the way I would. She was truly swift and decisive. Besides, if he loved her the way he claimed, she would never have had to feel the pain and humiliation as she did before all those people.

What has been so exciting these past several weeks is how our bond has grown even stronger. I told her in the beginning that if I could erase anything from her past that has troubled her, and in a perfect world if it included erasing those motherfuckers from it, then that's exactly what I needed to do.

She merely smiled back at me, and the gleam in her eyes had said it all. Last night, she even confided in me that she was glad that she met me. She was glad to have someone like me handle her problems.

"A real man makes life easier for the woman," she told me.

Her words were both shocking and soothing. I was nearly overcome with so much emotion. All I could say was that I had a surprise for her. "It will be a celebration of our time together. I know it's not been long, but I feel the moment is right."

"What is it you have planned?"

"You'll see."

Tonight after she gets off work, I'm going to surprise her with a romantic dinner. Then I'll take her up to Malibu for a walk on the beach under the moonlight. Then I'll propose to her and forever dignify our love.

I better stop while I'm ahead. I'm not only feeling giddy but excited in a very sexual way. I'd rather not waste a nut on myself. I'd rather that it be expended the proper way, a culmination of true love and passion.

Chapter 18

Cole Kennedy
Westwood, California

I live about a mile and a half away from UCLA, not far from Wilshire Boulevard. Every morning, I'll stop at Starbucks for a latté and then make the five-minute drive to the campus. Sometimes when I'm not in such a rush, I enjoy the thirty minutes that it takes to walk on campus.

Like most mornings, I was running late and in serious need for a cup of coffee before the long day schedule. I was lucky to find a parking spot near the front door. I guess I was focused on other things because I swear I did not see him. I ran square into him knocking his briefcase and papers all over the ground.

"I'm sorry, I can't believe I wasn't looking." I immediately squatted to pick up the papers; he joined me, flashing me a pearly smile. My eyes met his seductive stare.

"It's okay. Are you always in a hurry?" His icy grey eyes burned a hole in my mind. I tried to shake the naughty thoughts that were forming in my mind. I handed him the last of the papers and stood.

He extended his hand. "Hello, I'm Stefan."

"Hi Stefan. My name is Cole." I gave him a firm handshake, making sure I made full eye contact. He opened the door and followed me inside Starbucks. We placed our orders and waited at a nearby table.

He told me that he was new to the area. He found a place just off Sawtelle, which was near the Veteran's Hospital and not far from my Purdue Street apartment.

"I've been so busy adjusting to my new job, that I haven't been able to explore this beautiful city," he said. "Would you happen to know a place where I can have a nice dinner?"

"L.A. can be overwhelming, I know. I've been here four years and I'm still finding some of the best-kept secrets tucked in unexpected places."

I flashed him a smile. He was rather good looking. He reminded me of the former Lakers basketball player who married Vanessa Williams. His tanned complexion made him glow in the morning sunlight. He looked at me so attentive and engaging. His jet black hair was short and sharp. He was reasonably well dressed.

The clerk at the counter called my order number; I quickly retrieved my order and returned to the table.

"Stefan, it was a pleasure speaking to you. I hope you make enough time to venture out and explore the city."

"I would love for you to show me around."

He handed me his business card: Stefan Lewis, regional sales representative for Arctic Pharmaceutical. I was impressed; he couldn't have been that much older than me.

"If my hectic schedule allows me to, I would love to show you around." I took the card and stuffed it in my purse. Then I stood, exhaling loudly. "If I'm late again, my professor will kill me."

Stefan caught up with me just as I was about to open the door. "You're the first real person I connected with since arriving riving here. And I hope I'm not being too forward, but I really would like to see you tonight. Maybe I can take you out to dinner?"

He had a sad puppy dog look in his eyes. There was a seductiveness about him that stirred something in me that I had not considered since Kavion.

"Okay, there's a newfound favorite spot of mine in Little Tokyo. Only if I'm not too tired from school." I gave him a sly wink and walked away.

* * *

I had not been in the company of a man since Kavion. Humph, for that matter, I had not even thought about a man's attention save for a few personal moments that consisted of me and my bullet vibrator. School had consumed most of my social life. This was my last semester and the most stressful.

The rest of my day was uneventful. I could not wait to get home since I had a lot to do before my date with Stefan. Then I ran into him at the grocery store on my way home.

"Well, what a coincidence that we'd see each other again, Cole," he said, with a look of excitement that was unsettling.

That suspicion was confirmed when I accepted the offer to shake his hand. He made my skin crawl at that moment, causing my creeper antenna to be at a high-reception alert.

"Yeah, uh, I guess it's my lucky day to see you," I responded. "I'm in a bit of a hurry to take care of a few things before I see you later on today."

"Sure thing. Just seeing you has really made my day. See you later—"

I knew that I could not go out with him. Because of the bad vibe that I received, I decided instead to spend the evening snuggled up on my sofa nursing a pint of Chunky Monkey Ben & Jerry's ice cream and laughing my ass off at Craig and Smokey on Friday the movie.

The following week, which was a Saturday, I walked into the lobby only to find Stefan sitting in one of the chairs with a beautiful bouquet of white lilies and red roses. I was cautious as I walked up to him. My intuition warned me that I should run the other way, hop over the fence and never look back, but I was still curious.

As I walked closer to him, he began to rise, holding the flowers as a peace offering.

"For me?"

I accepted the flowers and read the card:

I am thinking of you . . . You are on my mind . . . You are in my heart.

I swallowed hard to contain my true feelings of fear. Fear that Stefan might not be the person I spoke to last week. Fear that he might be a little unstable. So, I gently place the flowers on a nearby table. I sat across from him, staring at him intently. There was something vague about his eyes. He turned slightly, breaking the silence.

"I wanted to see you again," he said.

He rubbed his hand nervously. He also seemed fidgety and preoccupied so much that it made me nervous.

"I apologize for not calling. I had a hectic week," I said. "And, uh, how did you know where I stayed?" I had a weird feeling he knew more about me than he portrayed.

"Yesterday, I was leaving a friend's house down the street and thought I saw you enter the lobby and took a leap of faith." There was a Cheshire cat-like grin that crept over his face. Even more telling was the sweat that began forming on his forehead.

"About the other day, really, it was a coincidence we met at the grocery store and I know how this may look . . . I had a group meeting in the area that lasted longer than I expected."

There was no doubt in my mind that bumping into Stefan was not a coincidence.

"Can I ask you another question?"

He shook his head inviting me to proceed. He also sat back in the seat appearing as if he had anticipated what I might ask.

"Have you ever sent me flowers to my job? I mean, I just needed to know if it was you. That was thoughtful and kind of you. I need to thank you for thinking of me."

I kept up the act in hopes of him opening up to me. I learned early on to keep a close eye on my enemy.

"There's so much I have to tell you, Cole," he answered, gushing with excitement. "Since the first day I saw you, I knew we were destined to be together." He looked longingly into my eyes, searching for the same sentiment. There was no way that I could match his, yet what he was telling me was incredulous.

"Stefan, I don't know what to say."

"Just tell me you feel the same." His look was desperate.

I shook my head, thinking of how I could end this conversation. "It has been a difficult year for me. It's just too soon for me to trust anybody right now."

"I know it's been hard, with the trial and then the acquittals, that's why I did what I did—"

Call it coincidence. Maybe it was divine intervention.

"Cole Kennedy, I should pimp-slap your ass!"

Sydney's phone call was the best thing that could have happened to me. It had been several weeks since we reconciled and I last spoken to her.

"Hey girl, can you give me just one moment?"

I reminded myself that I owed her one, and I did not know how long I could keep the charade with Stefan.

"Stefan, I'm sorry. But this is a long-time friend of mine whom I'm supposed to be picking up at the airport. I should have already left. I need to be leaving right now."

I could not leave him fast enough. I sprinted for the elevator and quickly boarded it, pressing the CLOSE button several times before it complied. Once I reached my floor, I ran to my apartment and slammed the door shut. I bolted the chain and double-checked the locks and windows, making sure they were secure. I wanted to leave no chance that he could get into my place.

What the fuck just happened? I asked myself while I tried calming down.

Then it hit me just as sharply as being the recipient of bad news: I'm sure Stefan had something to do with Barry's death.

I searched for Detective Ramirez's card. After locating it at the bottom of the junkyard—my purse—I was apprehensive to call his number. He picked up his line just as I was about to change my mind.

"Ramirez," his deep baritone resonated through the phone.

I swallowed hard. "Hello, Detective Ramirez, this is Cole Kennedy. I think I have some information regarding someone who may be a person of interest in Barry Kinloch's murder."

"Is that right?"

"Oh, I'm very sure."

"I'm interested in any possible lead."

"I just spoke to someone—his name is Stefan Lewis—and he may have had something to do with Barry's death."

"Did he admit to killing him?"

"No, he did not straight-out and say he killed Barry. But he made it perfectly clear to me that he was responsible for what happened."

Detective Ramirez exhaled through his nose. "Miss Kennedy, no judge is going to issue out a warrant just because you think someone is the perpetrator. We need cold, hard evidence. We need hard proof."

Being a law student, I more than understood his rationale. Yet the bad feeling that I had for Stefan was even more compelling at the moment.

"Detective, what do you think he meant when he said, 'If the law could not protect you, then it was up to me to make it right by you?' "

"Ms. Kennedy, I'm not trying to dismiss what you said. That is still not considered hard evidence. That could be picked apart by any lawyer worth his or her salt and be presented to any jury as mere fabrication. Have you heard of the term Field of Distortion?"

Now I knew why I was so apprehensive, bordering cynical. These people can approach me based on circumstantial information; however, when they're being approached it's met by lethargy.

Despite the frustration and frantic nature of my phone call, all of the pieces of the puzzle were coming together. Everything made sense to me as the last several months flashed through my mind.

"Detective Ramirez, let me try again. I started getting flowers a couple of months following the verdict from an anonymous person," I explained. "This anonymous person, this guy, knows where I stay, where I work . . . he even knows when I'll be at Starbucks.

"All this time, he's been lurking in the shadows watching me and waiting for a chance to emerge. God only knows how long he's been watching me."

"All right, so you've had somebody send you flowers. Now you're thinking someone's been keeping tabs on you rather strategically?" The tone in Ramirez's voice seemed to convey sarcasm.

"Listen, Detective. I didn't call you to be treated like this. I didn't kill Barry. That's why I'm calling you. I believe there could be more to his murder as well as Anthony Holmes' accident than we're led to believe. But more importantly, I think Jamil Holdings is now in danger."

It seemed that I finally got somewhere with Ramirez. He was not as quick to snap back at me with some canned police bullshit.

"Okay, I will talk to my partner. But I can't promise you anything."

I exhaled in relief. "All I'm asking is to check him out." I gave Detective Ramirez the information from Stefan's business card, which is where he supposed to have worked since last year. I also heard him scribbling the information on a notepad.

"If this Stefan is as dangerous as you claim, you make sure you watch your back. And if he spooks you in any way, call me anytime."

"Thanks, Detective Ramirez."

It was nice to know someone legitimately was looking out for me, yet I still hung up the phone more confused and scared than I'd ever been.

Chapter 19

Stefan Lewis
Los Angeles, California

After Cole did not call, I felt as if I would be going out of my mind. We made plans to meet at Yutaka's in Little Tokyo. I sat there waiting for her for over forty-five minutes.

I kept telling myself that she was on the way. Each time I saw a car turning into the parking lot, I was convinced that she would be the person emerging from it. It never happened.

Embarrassed, I lost my appetite and I left. I had an even worse feeling once I made it back to my place.

"I'm sorry, Stefan. But classes were really, really rough today and I've had to do extra work so that I can keep up. I didn't realize how late it was until a couple of minutes ago . . . Can we meet another time?"

I did not want to believe that Cole did this to me—and to us. I spent the entire night replaying how we interacted earlier today. It had to have been when we ran into each other at the supermarket. I now recall seeing the baffled look of confusion in her eyes, questioning me without saying anything. I thought I played it off by pretending I did not see her, but she knew.

So what am I to do?

The thought of Cole as a no-show played prominently on my mind as I woke up this morning. My heart longed for her and I felt it was important that I saw her. I needed to see her smile because it just might help me make it through the day.

So, I decided to meet her in her apartment lobby. When she showed up, her mouth almost dropped to the floor; she was quick to regain her bearings.

"Stefan?" she asked.

My heart was encouraged as she accepted the bouquet of white lilies and red roses the florist called Always and Forever; it was a perfect expression of our love for each other.

"I hope I did not scare you off."

"Oh, it's nothing like that."

"I was really worried about us, uh, I mean you . . . I hope somebody else was the reason why you canceled our dinner date—"

"Really, Stefan, I was studying." She seemed rather calm with her response. For her sake, though, I hope that it's true, because if she was out with someone else I can't say what I would do.

The moment was fast becoming awkward. I was hoping that she might invite me up into her apartment. After all, I had been a perfect gentleman all these months since we've been going out. Not once had I forced the issue about any showing of affection, or dare I even say . . . sex.

Just as I was about to break the ice, our conversation was interrupted. She mentioned someone named Sydney, a long-time friend of hers, was on the line.

I had not heard much about her during our time together other than the fact she might not be somebody who's had Cole's best interests at heart like me. But I was not miffed at all when it appeared that Sydney had Cole's attention for the moment. What mattered was Cole would be mine for a lifetime.

"Stefan, I'm sorry . . . But I really need to be leaving right now," she told me.

"Sure, but I am glad that we saw each other. You just don't know what it meant."

In relationships, I've come to realize if a person truly loves someone, that person may have to do whatever it takes to make it work. And I've wanted so badly for our relationship to last. I realize what I've needed to do was convey to Cole just how much she's been the rock in my life just as I've been her protector.

At some point, she'll need to understand just how much we've been destined to be together, and nobody will ever step in between true love.

Chapter 20

Cole Kennedy
Los Angeles, California

Sydney has it going on when it comes to material things and living the lavish life—I could only dream about it. Even with daddy's money, it has still never amounted to the success she's had with Caramella Girl.

Normally whenever Sydney's asked me to hang out with her, I've declined because I've not wanted people to associate me as one of her girls—an escort or someone that would have sex for money.

Sydney and I have had many debates on this issue, and tonight was no different. I argued that she's still getting paid to have sex with these guys, and she's still considered a prostitute in the eyes of our society.

That merely provoked Sydney to give another of her animated rebuttals. While on the other line, I envisioned her wagging her finger and assuming a Queen Bitch pose.

"First of all, I'm not a gutter hoe. You'll never see me on the corner or in some back alley waiting for a cheap ass bum to offer twenty for a blowjob."

"So what's really the difference?" I retorted. "I don't see any."

"Girl, at least I get paid and I mean get paid. I am dating lawyers and doctors and movie stars. In case you haven't noticed, I look damn good. Who wouldn't want to be like me?"

She had a point, a good one at that.

Whenever we've gone out, I've seen countless numbers of men stop and simply gawk and shake their heads after getting a good look at Sydney. She has a slender face with a beauty mole just above her small lips. She likes wearing her hair long and flowing. She often wears hip-hugging dresses or jeans. And she loves to give hints of her cleavage.

"I'm dining at fine ass restaurants damn near every night experiencing the good life, and I am paid to look pretty for a rich motherfucker," she went on to say. "And it's not always about fucking, anyway. But if I do decide to fuck, he knows I'm not fucking for free."

She then snapped her finger. "Girl, you better get some of this money while it's hot, because I have you to know my calendar is filling fast and I'd love for you to hop on board."

I reminded her that I've got goals and aspirations, and they don't include fucking for a living. Ever since I was a young girl, I knew I was going to be an attorney. I loved watching every television show related to law. Law and Order and The Practice were among my favorites.

"Suit yourself. If it's a good night, we can easily make three thousand. It could be more," she said, hinting also I could make more depending on how far I'm willing to go.

"No, never."

"All I'll say is tonight is different. I'm not expected to fuck. I'm only enjoying a night on the town."

I paced back and forth on my patio observing how the sunrays had turned the sky into stunning shades of pink and purple, colliding against the horizon creating a beautiful canvas of love and passion.

Damn, I wish Kavion was here. I would have been relaxing with him and licking whipped cream off his sexy body. Instead, I'm worried that some crazy, delusional stalker might be lurking in the shadows. Scared that at any moment he would be ready to pounce or maybe kill me.

I decided against my better judgment to hang out with Sydney, who indicated that she was about twenty-five minutes away. "I'll meet you out front."

A black Lincoln Continental with dark-tinted windows slowly turned onto my street. The headlights were blinding, and they caused me to block the beams from my eyes. Just as it slowed, the back passenger window lowered and Sydney popped her big ass head out the window.

"Girl, you wearing the fuck out of that dress," she hollered; she also rushed out of the vehicle and gave me a hug. "Imma have to keep you away from Akeno tonight."

She turned around and began clapping her ass cheeks. It was equally tempting to give her a playful smack. "Because one look at you and he might forget about this booty."

Once inside her luxury ride, I was informed that we would be going to the Bungalow Club on Melrose Drive, and my date's name was Gabriel—I returned her a concerned look.

"Trust me, you are going to have a wonderful time with Gabe," she said. "Just think of it as a blind date that just so happens to be fine as aged wine, sexy as hell, and loaded out the ying-yang."

She paused and looked me over. "If you play your cards right, you will have Gabe eating out the palm of your hand. Maybe he'll have you forgetting about Kavion."

I swallowed hard and loud, looking straight ahead. "I don't know what you told him about me. But I'm warning you, if I'm not feeling him, he won't get pass first base." Then I turned and faced her. "And I sure as hell am not fucking him. I don't care if he looks like Blair Underwood or Shamar Moore. "

We both laughed at that remark.

Fifteen minutes later, we arrived at the Bungalow Club. The restaurant offered a beautiful Moroccan atmosphere featuring burgundy walls, silk curtains, candles and chandeliers. I was mesmerized by the restaurant's ambiance.

The hostess informed us that our party called and would be arriving in twenty minutes. She led us to the outside patio into one of the bungalows surrounded by burgundy and cream print silk curtains.

By the time Akeno and Gabriel arrived, I had already loosened up after a couple of lemon drop martinis. But I was able to maintain my composure when I stood up to accept Gabriel's handshake.

"Pleased to meet you, Ms. Cole Kennedy," he said.

"Thank you," I replied; I felt my body temperature rise and wetness between my legs. "I consider it a privilege and honor."

Clearly, I did not expect to meet someone as gorgeous as him. It was as if I'd seen a page from a fashion magazine come to life. I quickly learned that Gabriel was the son of one of Hollywood's hottest film directors, Sayid Andrews, and his mother was none other than fashion designer Tori Cabaret. I knew that Sydney was well-connected; I did not realize that she had these kinds of connections.

It took all of me not to act like a groupie because I was wearing a Tori Cabaret dress, and I was this close to one of my favorite designers.

"I've got to know how your father managed to deal with all those egos when he worked on the set of You Can't Handle It," I inquired. "I mean, he had Tom Crowe, John Newsome, Karl Sanderson, and Deana Morgan—all big names in their own right—and he got them to work together in a movie. That's impressive."

Gabriel chortled. "You just don't know what he went through. My mom said every night he had to convince himself to go back the next day on the set."

"I bet that was interesting. So tell me, how were you able to have any sort of a normal childhood with famous parents?" I asked. "They've had such demanding careers."

"You're right. They have had demanding careers, but the best thing I can say is that they've always tried their best to make time for me. It might not have been easy for me to see it growing up, but looking back I can see where they tried."

Gabriel also told me that his parents were supportive of his interests in modeling and being a race car driver, which he said he does every chance he gets.

"You know, I feel like I'm being interviewed. Tell me a little more about yourself, Cole."

"I'll be graduating from UCLA law school in a couple of months, and my focus is entertainment law."

"Really?"

"Yes. So, uh, maybe you might need somebody to negotiate your next contract—"

"You never know."

Gabriel seemed impressed with my accomplishments and worldly endeavors after I also mentioned to him how extensive I've traveled abroad.

"I'm somewhat shocked because I thought you were—"

"An escort?"

His eyes answered the question. I shook my head. "My friend Sydney runs her own company, but I am not associated with it."

He reacted by picking up his drink, a pinot noir; it was more like a sense of relief. "It's not often you meet women who are ambitious and exude professionalism."

We continued our conversation straight through our tiramisu, arguing which bakery in Italy made the best. Maybe it was the four lemon drops or possibly the stimulating conversation. Whatever it was, I felt rather emboldened being his company.

"I've got nothing to do this evening. Perhaps we can finish this conversation over a nightcap?"

"Your place or mine?"

"How about yours?" I replied, with a seductive gaze.

Immediately, I considered that I had not been with anyone since Kavion, and that had now been more than seven months. But I had never been with anyone of Gabriel's celebrity status.

I glanced over at Sydney's table. I did not need any further convincing. She seemed so much in her element. Yet I recognized there was some truth to her philosophy.

She once said, "A man takes you out to dinner and a movie, fifty dollars tops he's spent. You go back to your place, or his, you lay down with him and you've given it up for a happy meal."

Then I remembered her bragging that she may or may not fuck, but she'd still go home having made no less than three grand. Another of her famous sayings resonated within me: "Now tell me who's really the fool?"

Although her lifestyle's been something I've always been curious of, I still cannot fathom having sex for money.

I'm grown, and I can fuck whomever I want, I said to myself. She can call me a fool, but I will still wake up with my dignity. Who am I to judge? That way of life is definitely not for me.

* * *

My bladder was past full. I excused myself to go to the rest room. I navigated my way through the restaurant and adjusted my eyes towards the direction of the women's bathroom.

Just as I entered, I heard someone behind me and the door being locked. I turned around startled to be face to face with Stefan.

I was drunk but not that inebriated that I did not know something was definitely wrong with this man, and that he was without a doubt following me.

"What are you doing? This is the women's rest room. Why are you following me, Stefan?" I was beyond pissed off. Creeping behind bushes. Lurking in the fucking shadows. And to think, I only bumped into him last week.

"You have to be following me to know I was here. So how did you know that I was here?" I was determined that he was going to answer me, damnit.

He searched hard for something to say. He spoke barely above a whisper. "Cole, it's not like that—"

"So was the meeting at the coffee shop an accident or did you stage that, too?" I interrupted him.

"Cole you've got me all wrong. Have I done anything wrong? I just do not want you to make another mistake. I'm only looking out for you."

I placed my hands on my hips, rolling my neck. "A mistake? You don't even know me well enough to come to that conclusion."

"Seven months is a long time. I was just giving you space. I know how hard it has been for you lately . . . the rape, the acquittals, losing your mother the way you did . . ."

So this motherfucker does know everything about me. I was feeling provoked to cock my hand and punch him hard in the fucking mouth. "How do you know anything about my mother or my life?"

His grey eyes that seemed to be lost and in a gaze were now marble-size black coals.

"Cole, we were meant for each other; and when two people are in love, nothing, and I mean nothing, can ever come between that."

"I'm not in love with you." I retorted.

"Not yet, but you will be. You know you love how I made you feel. How I seduced your mind and body—I bet you're creaming just thinking about me right now."

He grabbed both my hands and placed them loosely on his shoulders. Then he licked the side of my cheek. "Mmm, you smell so good and you taste so sweet," he moaned. "I bet your pussy tastes and smells the same way."

I was shaken in my stilettos but I kept my cool. I wondered why some of the most beautiful people in the world had the biggest problems. What a waste on such a beautiful looking man.

"Don't go home with him, Cole," he begged, staring blankly at me. This man had become a shell of a person. It was as if I had a glimpse of the evil within.

"I have only one more loose end to tie up and then we'll be together. I made a promise to you, and I intend to make it right by you."

He now managed a wisp of a smile. Before I could react, he kissed my cheek where he licked. Then he turned around and left, whistling an eerie tune. His mannerisms were as if he was the luckiest man in the world.

I wiped away his saliva and began sobbing. Instinctively, I dashed towards the sink and began vigorously washing his scent off my face. After all the shit I'd been through, I'd always felt that I was a strong person, but this was too much for me to handle.

Through my tears, I glanced into the mirror. I did not like what I'd seen. I felt my legs giving away from me as I crumbled to the floor. What did I do to deserve this turmoil in my life? How can I rid myself from a lunatic without losing my own life?

Chapter 21

Sydney Starks
Los Angeles, California

I was so wrapped up in my conversation with Akeno that I did not recognize that Cole had been away from her table for a long time.

"Hey, do you know what's with your girl?" Akeno asked. "I noticed Gabriel's been over there alone. Do you think she called a cab or something?"

"Cole isn't like that. She won't just up and leave somebody unless there's a reason. And from what I noticed, it seemed that they were getting along."

"Are you sure about that?"

I checked my watch and decided that I'd give her five more minutes before I personally searched for her. Time is money. And keeping somebody as fine as Gabriel waiting was unacceptable even if she was doing this as a favor for me.

Inwardly, I hoped she was not in the bathroom hurling her insides out or had passed out after all those damn lemon drops that she downed like candy earlier. But I was in no mood to be babysitting a grown ass woman. Handling one's liquor is one of the first things that I tell my girls when they're out with their clients. I demand for them to be on their A-game at all times, and I still would expect that from Cole.

My concern for Cole got the best of me, however.

"Akeno, would you excuse me for a moment?" I said.

The head waiter told me that he recalled seeing someone that fit Cole's description walking towards the bathrooms, so that was the first place I checked. No sooner than I stepped inside, I found her in the fetal position in the corner, sobbing.

"Cole, what's wrong? I asked.

She could not even form the words. So I checked the bathroom stalls to assess if there was anything that happened in any of them. They were empty, clean in fact. I rushed back to her.

"Cole, talk to me, girl. Tell me what happened?"

She looked up at me. "Some crazy guy has been stalking me," she said between sobs. "He followed us here to the restaurant tonight."

"What did he look like?"

"It doesn't matter. We need to call Detective Ramirez. He'll know what to do."

"Where is his number?"

Cole closed her eyes and shook her head. She was out of it. I had never seen Cole like this. Her make-up was smeared. Her face appeared as if she bore the world's burdens, including hers. She seemed exhausted by the encounter.

Not knowing what else to do, I wrestled Cole's purse out of her grasp and scoured through it. She had so much shit in it that I practically had to dump all the contents on the floor before I discovered a business card with a policeman's name on it.

Humph, of all things. Me talking to somebody from law enforcement?

I took a deep breath and calmed myself while I waited for somebody to answer.

"Detective Ramirez, may I help you?" There was no doubt that he was a Latino with his accent. I began envisioning somebody with dark hair and possibly tanned.

"Officer, my cousin Cole Kennedy says that she's spoken to you before," I answered, pacing the floor. "I'm with her right now at a restaurant and she was traumatized by somebody who's been stalking her. Can you help?"

"Do I need to dispatch somebody over there immediately?"

"No, I don't think that's necessary."

"Okay, I'll tell you what. I'm in the middle of completing a report that has to be on my captain's desk in about thirty minutes." He paused quickly.

"I'll tell you what. Can you meet us at her place?" I suggested. "We're not far from there."

"I know where it is."

I walked back over to Cole, who was now sitting up with her back against the wall. "Listen here, girl, you need to get yourself together. I'm taking you back home. Detective Ramirez said he'll meet us there in an hour."

"Thank you so much, Sydney," she said, sniffling.

"I'll go outside and let Akeno and Gabriel know that you're all right."

I found Akeno and Gabriel near the bar talking to two very attractive women that wore outfits that left little to the imagination. Being the businessperson that I am, I saw this as an opportunity to see if they had what it took to carry the Caramella Girl name; and besides, I needed to keep competition away from what I claimed was mine.

When I was within an earshot, Gabriel immediately asked about Cole's well-being. At least I knew my girl could keep a man's attention.

"She'll be okay. She was hit with a sudden case of the stomach bug. She gives her regards."

We embraced. I noted the smell of citrus and a hint of sandalwood. I was sure he wore a fragrance by Hugo Boss.

"Well, tell her to give me a call when she's feeling better. I would love to continue our conversation." He gave me his business card and wrote his private number on the back.

While giving him a goodbye hug, I whispered in Akeno's ear that I would call him later tonight so we could finish what we started.

* * *

The ride back to Cole's place was uneventful. She did not utter a single word the entire trip. I walked her to her door, helped her inside, and made sure that she was safe. I even checked the closet in her bedroom and the other rooms.

"Think you can make it through the night?" I asked.

"Sydney, thank you for everything. I hope I did not ruin your night with Akeno. How was Gabriel?"

I sat down next to Cole and gave her a hug. "Girl, don't worry about it. Gabriel wants to see you again. He was really concerned—he even gave you his personal number." I was quick to search my purse and handed it to her.

My mind was going in several different directions. Part of me wanted to get back to Akeno. I wanted to console my friend, but I also wanted to know what really happened back at the restaurant.

"Do you want to talk about what happened earlier? Who is this guy and what did you do to have him stalking you?"

Cole buried her head in her hand, shaking it. "The guy is weird, crazy. And I did nothing to provoke him into following me."

"Come on now, girl. This is me. Your girl, Sydney. No man is going to follow a woman unless something happened between them."

I knew that I had gotten under Cole's skin, but I needed to know. It just seemed to be an all too common scenario, the, I'm-being-targeted-because-I'm-beautiful syndrome.

"Sydney, it's been a long night for me. I just want to go to sleep."

"Sure, you do that," I said. "As for me, I've got business to take care of."

After I left Cole's place, I could never buy that she's being stalked randomly. I was positive that she's been the cause of her own problems.

Chapter 22

Stefan Lewis
Los Angeles, California

When Cole finally emerged from the rest room with Sydney, I felt compelled to run over and console her and dry any tears that she may have shed. I wanted to hold her in my arms and protect her from whoever had upset her—I wondered whether that sordid statement for a dinner date had said something wrong.

I mean, she appeared to be okay after I left her, and the feeling was definitely mutual. And to think, she actually passed up on some pretty boy actor for me. I'd never felt so respected by any woman.

I promise that I'll be good, she told me.

"You better, if you know what's good for you," I replied, jokingly.

Passion can be so kinetic; it does not take long for it to ignite. Just looking into Cole's eyes and touching her skin had me besides myself. I'd never been so giddy. No doubt, coming to Los Angeles was the best decision I could have made; I've found true love here in this city.

We made plans to see each other for dinner tomorrow night, and we sealed our commitment to each other with a kiss goodnight. I shuddered at the sensation of her tongue being entwined with mine. And I almost lost it right there in her presence when she groped and fondled me.

Suddenly, she withdrew.

"I'm not in love with you," she said.

I did not immediately understand. Then it dawned upon me that she's confused and sometimes falling in love does not come easy for some people. I explained to her that I had fallen in love with her the first moment I laid eyes on her.

That still had not registered with her. She returned a blank stare.

"It's all right. I don't mind giving you time," I told her. "You're worth the wait and while. I don't mind staying back and watching over you."

That is precisely what I've been doing. I stayed around long enough to know that she did not go home with him. She needs me to protect her because I know in due time the feeling will be mutual.

I left the restaurant just in time to see Cole and Sydney depart in the same black vehicle that they arrived in. Then I rushed to my car parked in the nearby garage and drove rather aggressively, weaving in and out of traffic until I caught up with them; they were a block in front of me.

Luckily for Cole, it appeared they were headed straight for her apartment. I wanted to be sure that a particular individual who resembled a suave movie star did not show up for any midnight snack. So, I sat across the street from her lobby entrance until two o'clock in the morning.

I was more than satisfied that Cole was willing to respect our relationship. That alone took it to another level. Impressed, I decided that I would dial her number.

"Hello?"

Her voice was so angelic in my ear that the sound of her voice rendered me speechless. I quickly hung up; however, I sat there enthralled with the phone glued to my ear long after the dial tone stopped.

Damn, the woman had stolen my breath—and much more.

Chapter 23

Cole Kennedy
Los Angeles, California

It turned out that Detective Ramirez did not show up as he had promised, leaving me to spend the night sleeping on the living room sofa and worried that this nutcase named Stefan might show up again.

The most frightening thing about this was knowing that someone else whom I'd never met before was knowledgeable of some of the most intimate details about my personal life. He even knew that my mother was deceased.

And it's not as if I'd gotten over my mother's death. So much was lost, and very little healing has since followed. Now it was happening to me again.

Just as I was about to sink into a pity party for myself, I was startled by my phone going off. My heart began racing. Stefan's voice was the last thing I needed to hear again. I ended up not answering. The phone went off again. There was still no way that I'd answer.

About ten minutes later, I heard knocking on the door. I began to tremble a bit. Cautiously, I approached the peep hole and peered through it.

"Who is it?" I inquired.

"It's Detective Ramirez."

I could not easily discern the male standing outside. "How do I know it's you?"

"Ms. Kennedy, I'll show you my badge and ID," he answered. "Uh, could you at least open your door so that I can show it?"

I finally recognized Detective Ramirez's accent, so I felt fairly comfortable that Stefan would not be on the other side.

"Just a minute." I fumbled to unlatch the door and unlock it. I actually breathed a sigh of relief once our eyes met.

"Good morning. Sorry about last night. I should have called, but our daughter had a bronchitis attack. We had to take her to Kaiser."

Ramirez wore a black shirt and dark slacks. His badge was on his right front pant pocket. I was glad that he was not accompanied by his partner, Detective Jenkins. But I was disappointed to know that he was apparently a married man with a family.

"You look like you may have been there all night," I said.

He nodded. "Close to it. Now I know what some of the victims we see go through on a Friday night. I've had maybe two hours' sleep."

"That's about how much sleep I had."

I invited Detective Ramirez inside and showed him the sofa. I sat across from him in my recliner.

"You say that this guy has been following you, and he followed you into the ladies' room?"

"Yes, that's right." I began considering thoughts whether that was any form of harassment. "I couldn't believe that he did it. Is there anything that you can do about it?"

Detective Ramirez opened his notepad and began scribbling down what I told him. "Do you mind if I ask you a few questions?"

Sighing, I replied, "I hope they lead to something substantive."

At that moment, I recalled the hell my parents went through with Terri. She was so deranged after my father broke off their affair. I'm still not sure whether my father had come to his senses after realizing that he might have gone through a mid-life crisis, or maybe he realized something else about her.

What we do know was that she called him hundreds of times and left scary messages like she was going to kill him. Then she'd turn around and beg him to take her back. She followed my mother when she went shopping and to the university where she taught.

It got so bad that my mother took an indefinite leave of absence because of the constant harassment. It only ended when Terri was caught on tape vandalizing my mother's car. She was then arrested.

Stefan had not gone that far, but who knows? "Let me share this with you real quickly, Detective Ramirez. The guy who's been following me said that he had one more thing to take care of.

"I told you this before, but have you not noticed that there is only one of my attackers still alive?"

He tapped his notepad with his pen. "I did some research on your case, and you're right there is some correlation to what you've told me. We've actually considered this guy, uh, what's his name?"

"Stefan. Stefan Lewis." I paused and retrieved my purse. His business card was still inside. "Here, this is the card that he gave me."

"How long ago was that?"

"About a little over a week ago."

"Can you give me a description of how he looks?"

I set aside my disdain for even the thought of Stefan to describe that he had rather handsome features, and that he stood about five-nine and weighed probably one hundred and eighty pounds.

"Are you aware of what kind of car he drives?"

I shook my head. "I only seen him twice before last night. Each time, I happened to walk somewhere and he was already there."

"Ms. Kennedy, if we were to find him, would you be able to identify him in a line up?"

"Absolutely."

Detective Ramirez instructed me if Stefan showed up not to approach him, but call the police department at once. He also said that he would conduct surveillance near my home, and he would have a patrol unit drive by my area for any suspicious persons.

Finally, I felt at ease knowing that someone was watching out for me.

Chapter 24

Stefan Lewis
Los Angeles, California

Today is the day, and it's no accident that I've chosen it to complete my mission.

One year ago today, Cole Kennedy was raped by three monsters. She was denied justice by the jury of her peers, but she has since found solace in a stable relationship with someone who loves her dearly.

Now, the message must be sent that nobody will ever hurt my baby.

That's right. One motherfucker to go.

I'd be surprised if Jamil Holdings remembers exactly what he did a year ago this day. He was the one who forced Cole to suck his dick while Barry Kinloch fucked her from behind. Just like the other two, Jamil never showed any contrition for his despicable deed after the trial. He bragged often how women could and would not resist him.

Not surprisingly, Jamil happened to choose this day to have his ego stroked, if not more, by one of his periodic trips to the Fantasy Gentleman's Club not far from the Sunset Strip.

He's definitely the sickest of the three. Society needs to be rid of this psychopath.

I've watched Jamil long enough to know that he's had an addiction, which is often satiated for the moment by whores who parade around him with their asses out and doing things with their orifices that are not normal or sanitary.

The first one who caught his attention tonight was Exotica, a dark complexion big booty beauty. Her slant eyes reminded me of a Polynesian hula dancer. While the DJ played a popular song by a group named Silk—"Freak you up and down"—I actually enjoyed the way Exotica swayed her hips to the music.

I can't really say it's too bad she's not like the love of my life, Cole, I said to myself. But I'd better not allow my mind to wander too far. I must be true to her, and for her.

Intent on carrying out my mission, I made my way closer to where Jamil sat—he was about three tables away from the stage. Then between sets, I followed him to the bar; it was also where I began to execute things.

"Excuse me, please don't take this the wrong way," I started with Jamil; I rubbed my chin as if I was in deep recollection. "But you do look awfully familiar to me."

I then snapped my finger just as the bartender, a rather attractive female with short hair stopped by. "I know where I recognize you. It was in the NCAA tournament game—"

He looked at me from the corner of his eye, but he stuck his chest out. I learned a while back assholes like him always looked for adoration.

"What is it you'll have?" the bartender interrupted me; she was much the aggressive type.

"I'll have another Coke and rum, thank you."

I turned my attention back to Jamil. "You were clearly the best player. I felt you should have been named the game's MVP. Now I know why they call you the name they call you."

"You mean 'The Jugular'?" he responded.

"Yeah, that's it. You're definitely take no prisoners."

The bartender returned with my drink. She then nodded in Jamil's direction.

"Tonight's your lucky night," I declared. "Whatever my man wants is on me."

I reached into my pocket and slapped a twenty on the counter the bartender, whom I also suspected was a lesbian, looked at Jamil once again.

"I'll just have a Corona with lime."

"Great choice." I also flagged a waitress who happened to pass by. "Make sure you take care of my man here. Whatever he wants." I paused and winked at her. "I got it."

Jamil took his bottle back to his table. This was the side of the establishment where the artistic side of the freaks took center stage. This was where live fantasies become reality.

The DJ introduced Sajoya with a mix of music that combined a popular song titled "Still DRE" with some Middle Eastern flair. Jamil could not control himself. He howled as if he was a werewolf.

Perhaps there was good reason. Sajoya was fair complexioned. Her partially hidden eyes made her appear as if she was a feline on the prowl. She wore a baby blue Arabian belly dancer's costume. She was tall, quite possibly six feet, and marvelously stacked.

Within moments, it was clearly evident that her performance would captivate the audience. Her routine began like a slow dance, grinding and rocking as the music gained momentum. Her flexibility made her belly dancing skills even more mesmerizing. But it was her erotic self-pleasuring moves that took her routine to another level. I had to remind myself that I was a faithful man. Meanwhile, Jamil had flung a handful of money out on the stage.

Towards the end of her routine, Sajoya wore only gold nipple tassels—a man could have been hypnotized had he decided to follow her breasts while she shook her body—and string for a bikini.

Sajoya had much potential to help a man whose dick was hard as a brick and in dire need of releasing any cum pent up inside him. But I was not that person. I reminded myself that I had saved mine for Cole, and I've got every reason to believe that we'd consummate our relationship much sooner than later.

Apparently, Sajoya's performance was too much for Jamil to handle. I noticed that he was walking towards the bathroom. He had one hand in his pocket possibly to hide his erection. I eagerly waited for him to reappear. At that moment, I motioned for the waitress to refill his drink, if he was ready.

I noticed that he shook his head, and he began walking towards the front door. That was my cue to catch up—fast. I could not let this opportunity escape.

God had to have been with me. There was a bit of a logjam at the front door with people coming in and leaving, and that allowed me to be within a couple of steps of Jamil once he started walking outside. The streets, too, were surprisingly clear and he never looked behind while he walked along the outer sidewalk. I still tried to look natural and as non-suspicious as possible before I made my move.

That occurred the moment he reached the end of the building. I raced up behind him, turned him around by his collar, and elbowed him in the mouth.

"What the fuck?" he said, wide-eyed; his reactions were slowed by all that liquor he consumed inside the establishment.

I jacked him against the building, gave him a knee in the mid-section, and elbowed him again in the mouth. Then I pulled out a large switchblade and held it against his throat. He seemed to be temporarily paralyzed by fear.

"Nobody hurts my fiancée and gets away with it. Do you know what today is, huh punk? "I snarled.

"What the fuck are you talking about?" He attempted to break free, but I pressed the switchblade harder. I figured if he was stupid to risk an artery being cut, so be it.

Now I was the one in control. I was the one who was exerting power. In my rage, I kicked him in the groin. But I did not allow him to drop to his knee. Immediately, I pushed him against the building.

"You're some fucking man, aren't you?" I said through gritted teeth. "You shove your dick in a woman's mouth while the other one's raping her?"

"I don't know what the fuck you're talking about."

Denial. That sent me into a rage. "You'll know what the hell I'm talking about, motherfucker!"

I decided that this bastard needed to understand that water was wet. So, I grazed his chest with the tip of the blade while I ripped a hole through his shirt. He damned near choked once he realized that he sustained a superficial cut; I also noticed that his breathing had quickened.

"Look, you can have my money. Just . . . just—"

"Shut the fuck up!"

I was poised to eviscerate this bastard when I heard what had to have been vagrants nearby fussing with one another.

"How come every time I buy the liquor you end up holding the bottle like it's yours?" one of them yelled.

Damn, I knew that I could not have any witnesses. So I yelled, "Hey, take your shit somewhere else!"

"Fuck you," I heard another voice retort.

Apparently, I told them where they could go, because they walked off. But shit, I wished that I had not allowed myself to be sidetracked because Jamil knocked the knife out of my hand.

Instinctively, I grabbed onto his shirt as he tried tackling me onto the ground. I heard a loud thud, which was my head when it hit the asphalt; I refused to give into the pain or possibly blacking out.

Somehow as we tussled, I managed to regain the upper hand and locate my knife. This time, I was determined to end things quickly.

In an instant, I raised the knife to Jamil's throat. His eyes grew as big as saucers. This was a fitting expression for the crime that he committed against my lady.

"Freeze. Put down your weapon now!" I heard someone behind me say.

I picked up from the corner of my eye someone hovering over me. His gun was drawn; he was at point-blank range.

"I said put down your weapon!"

I turned slightly to my right. The first thing that I picked up on was his badge hanging outside his pant pocket. He looked rather grimy as if he may have been one of those vagrants that had tussled just earlier.

"Do you not understand, put down your weapon!"

The other person also appeared now right in front of me with his gun pointed. Damn. I'd been caught by the police. "Put your hands over your head!" His voice was familiar. He was the one who told me to go fuck myself. At this moment, I suppose that I was fucked.

I had only one choice, and that was to surrender. But I still thought of Cole and I being together. Suddenly, I felt my hands being forcefully placed behind me. Then I was pushed forward, face-first onto the asphalt.

Click-click!

I guess they meant business.

"You have the right to remain silent . . . Anything you say can be used against you in the court of law . . ."

The enormity of the moment had finally caught up with me. I was so overcome that I began feeling light-headed.

"What took you so fucking long?" I heard Jamil say; his voice was frantic. "I thought he was going to kill me."

He was right. That was also when I passed out.

Chapter 25

Cole Kennedy
Wednesday, January 2012
Charleston, South Carolina

I'd just returned to my plush corner office at Smith, Downey & Brown, eager to get started on my newest case. Before my assistant Jabree had any chance to say "hello," I was quick with making my demands.

What a lawyer's dream, I must say. He's hard working, knows his shit like the back of his hand, and he doesn't bitch when the work becomes too demanding.

"I need the Chesney file on my desk in ten minutes . . . And, get Monty on the phone now!"

Within moments, Jabree was knocking on my door. "Come in—"

He carried two coffee mugs and a brown expandable folder underneath his arm. The smell of the coffee was sweet, and the vanilla aroma made my mouth salivate.

"Good morning, Cole. Here is the Chesney file you asked for," Jabree said in his usual jovial tone. Today, he wore khaki chinos and a tan striped button-down Ralph Lauren shirt. He also wore dark brown Gucci loafers with no socks. He took his seat in front of my desk, and we discussed the agenda for today.

"Asa Payne is Monty Edwards' godson, and I think we've got our hands full with this case," I said. "I need you to pull up Florida statues—fucking up is not an option here. Do you think you can get the motion done today?"

"Yes, but I better start on it now; we have a full schedule today," he answered. "You have a conference call with Moffatt Weathersby in ten minutes. And Mrs. Charlene Chesney wants to come by the office, but I think a call will suffice. I'll let her know to expect your call."

Jabree rose from the chair. His muscular and lean body reminded me how much I've missed having a strong, virile body next to me in bed. I shook the naughty thought out of my mind. Years ago, I vowed that I would never mix business with pleasure ever again. Not even if it were with someone with as great of a body as his.

As if I needed any reminder, I found myself recalling how hard work and dedication got me where I am today, but it was something I almost lost because of careless indiscretions with a superior.

I had a brief affair with one of the managing partners, Brett Downey, during my second year as an associate. I thought it was just something to do at a time in my life when I was feeling down on myself.

We worked in the same practice area, which required us to take frequent business trips together to places like the Virgin Islands, Bahamas, and Las Vegas. No doubt, we worked on cases, but we always made time in each other's bedroom.

He wanted more than I did, but I decided to use his infatuation to my advantage. For example, he knew a developer and he got me to the top of the list for a new condominium prior to its construction. I had the privilege of designing my split-level overlooking the Charleston harbor on Daniel's Island. Since he was friends with the local Mercedes dealer he assisted me with getting my dream car, a red SLK 300, for an unbelievable price.

What seemed promising in upward mobility almost was derailed the night Brett hosted a birthday extravaganza with an early 1980s theme at his six-thousand square foot oceanfront mansion on the Isle of Palm.

I decided to attend the party with Teague Ricart, a sexy Dominican who was a rising star in the firm. In his first year, he made a name for himself when he won a high-profile case that involved him defending the estate of a mentally ill Latino man who was killed by a Charleston police officer.

Mr. Downey's wife, Deidra, surprised him with a surprise guest, The Gap Band, featuring lead singer Charlie Wilson and his brothers, Ronald and Robert. They sung all of their classic hits from that era, including "Burn Rubber on me," "You Dropped a Bomb on Me," and "Outstanding."

After the band's second set, I decided that I had enough of dodging Brett and keeping Teague away from all the interns, and I decided it was time to leave. I went to the coat room to retrieve my belongings when Deidra entered the room and approached me carrying a manila envelope.

She then gestured with her head as she handed it to me. "Go ahead, take a look inside. I've held on to it for a while now. I'm still not sure if I'll use them against Brett."

My hands became clammy and shaky, but the suspense was too much to avoid.

"You'll be shocked as I was when I received this hand delivered a couple of months ago."

She began walking towards a bar where she grabbed a shot glass and poured herself a shot of Louis XIII de Rémy Martin cognac. She downed it hard and slammed the glass on the granite surface.

I still had not opened the envelope.

"Go ahead," she insisted; she then poured herself another shot. She swirled it around in the glass before swallowing in a single gulp.

Brett told me that his wife drank a lot. Now I understood what he meant by her being nothing more than a lush. I was aware that he'd asked her to get help, but she always claimed that she did not have a problem.

So, I finally opened the envelop and pulled out four eight-by-ten color prints of me and her husband.

I barely kept a straight face. The pictures captured us fucking on my balcony overlooking the waterfront. His eyes were closed, his hands holding on to my ass, and I worked to match his strokes.

There was no way I could deny being with him. I remembered that night vividly. We had finished arguing about a recent romp I had with Teague.

"There's nothing you can really say. You're a married man, and you have no control over whom I entertain in my spare time," I told him.

He retorted, "You seem to forget who helped you get this place and that car you're driving."

I had long since learned and practiced the power of pussy. Good pussy could control the nature of the relationship. And it controlled a man by his balls; he cannot think with anything except what's between his legs.

"If you can't handle the fact that I'm young with needs, which something you can't always give me, then I suggest we end this thing now."

"You don't really mean that—"

I took a step closer and traced a line from his chest down to his dick, which responded immediately to my touch. He grabbed my ass cheeks and kissed me hard on my lips. Then he pushed his tongue inside my mouth. My clit began throbbing with anticipation. As if it was by second nature, I had pulled up my skirt and my thong to the side, and I felt his dick hitting all the familiar spots.

Her husband and I were enjoying our make-up sex. It was so intense. Maybe because he was not mine, that made him so damn irresistible. He was an athletic man who worked out every day, and he had great stamina. His boyish face was surrounded by his curly salt-and-pepper hair, which made him that much more desirable.

Deidra sighed. "Compared to me, I guess it helps having an ass and boobs like yours. My investigator even said from his vantage point it appeared Brett damned near rained cum from your balcony. You two should be in porn together."

I remained stoic, although I was tempted to retort that I was sure at some point she tasted my pussy on one of those rare occasions that Brett did fuck her. However, what I had not yet told her was that we called it quits for good not long after that confrontation-turned-sexcapade.

"I should post these fucking pictures all over the Internet," she rambled. "Then the whole world will know how much of a whore that you really are, and Brett's a sleazy motherfucker and son of a bitch."

I still had not offered any explanation. I did not want to talk myself into a bigger hole. I was angry—not at her but at myself for being involved with another woman's man. More so, I was embarrassed; it left me with no other option.

"Mrs. Downey, I know that I can never offer any explanation that could ever satisfy your many questions. But I'm sorry. It was a mistake, something I regret—"

"Woman to woman, I know why you're fucking my husband; I know the games you silly bitches play at the firm," she said, interrupting me.

She then got up close in my face, wagging her index finger not far from my nose. Her breath reeked with alcohol. It was horrible enough to make me sick in my stomach.

"You think you are the only one that made him stray? Honey, you are just one pretty face and wet pussy among many. But I guarantee you he will always come back to me. You have been in my home and you have been around my children. All I'm asking you is to respect me as his wife. I want you to leave my fucking husband alone."

She turned around and began walking away, leaving me feeling exposed and shamed.

"Next time, I won't be as friendly. Now get your shit and leave my home before I throw your trifling ass out!"

When I told Brett what happened, he was livid about his wife's actions and outraged that she hired an investigator; he also knew that divorce was not an option with her. He bragged that she would never trade in her plush lifestyle so that another woman might benefit from being his wife.

I was able to overcome the shame of being caught and dodge the humiliation that could have come with it. Luckily, the affair or confrontation never was made public.

Six years later, I proved to be indispensable to the firm. Making partner before I turned thirty-five was monumental for me. My hard work added $75 million to the firm's portfolio.

Jabree had suddenly turned around as if he'd forgotten something. Then he snapped his finger.

"Before I forget, you had a message from a Sydney Starks, She said she has some urgent news and for you to call her no matter how late it might be. I'll e-mail you her number when I get back to my desk."

"Thanks, Jabree."

I twirled around in my chair and looked out into the harbor. I thought I'd ran away from my past. When I left California ten years ago, I erased everything about my life prior to coming here to South Carolina.

Perplexed, I found myself just staring into my twenty-six inch computer monitor. My mind wandered all over the place because I could not imagine why Sydney would call me after all these years. Then it hit me like a Mack truck. I last spoke to her right before that crazy guy was arrested for attempted murder.

Humph, that was what I'd now considered ages ago. My life has changed for the good since then. I'm a much different person because of it.

"Mr. Weathersby is on the other line, I'm transferring now," Jabree said; the line clicked over.

"Moffatt," I said, reclining back in my office chair. He was the opposing attorney representing my client's soon-to-be ex, Tadd "The Rev" Chesney. He claimed in his filing for divorce irreconcilable differences. But the real problem was he couldn't keep his dick in his pants.

"Cole, I'll draw up the petition and can have them to you by the end of the day."

There was so much fucking arrogance in his voice. I could imagine him with his feet propped up on his desk sipping gourmet coffee. But I had a trick up my sleeve.

"I'm sorry Moffatt, but my client advised me that unless your client agreed to the terms she laid out we would proceed as planned."

"Are you willing to drag this thing out in court when we have a prenuptial agreement in place? Do I have to remind you that your client signed this pre-nup?" I heard papers shuffling in the background.

"It was he that broke the rules, not her," I countered. "She was there working long hours right along with him. Did he forget it was her connections that he used to get the contracts he has today? You and I both know she deserves a whole lot more than what is on that pre-nup. Your client is a piece of work."

Then I hit him with the coup de gras.

"I guess you were not aware of your client's extra-marital affairs? This alone voids the pre-nup, Moffatt."

"Quit bull shitting me, Cole. What are you talking about? And why is this the first time I'm hearing of this allegation. What proof do you have?"

"I wasn't expecting this either. It was just yesterday when my investigator forwarded some rather interesting photos of your client with several different women; it seems your client has an insatiable appetite for younger women," I answered. "Are you sitting at your desk?"

To prove this wasn't a bluff to cheat his client out of his money, I clicked the SEND button and e-mailed Moffatt three pictures of Tadd Chesney with three different women.

I went on to say, "She wants the apartment in New York City, as well as the vacation home in Hilton Head. She is entitled to the investments she's contributed to over the course of the years. Your client and his business are worth $300 million, and he can't do what's right by my client and give her what she's earned. She thus deserves the settlement amount of $75 million.

"Trust me, Moffatt, there are more where that came from. I don't think your client wants to play hardball here."

Now it was my turn to exude arrogance. My hands were clasped behind my head and my feet were propped on my desk awaiting Moffatt's response.

"He will be lucky to keep half his worth," Moffat said; it was apparent that he was trying to buy time. "I don't imagine he wants to humiliate himself, what will this do to his image as a pillar in this community?"

"Well, I can imagine how you must feel on this one. I will give you until Thursday morning to iron the particulars out with your client. I'm expecting an absolute agreement to the terms or we can continue this conversation in court."

The tone in my voice signaled that I was wrapping up this conversation. I knew that Moffatt was used to being the big man, barking orders and everyone jumped. Clearly, he was not prepared for this showdown that I devised. I was ecstatic I had him by the balls, and it took great restraint not to twist and squeeze them. I knew I could not show all my goodies before any commitment. That's why held back sending the fourth picture: Chesney with a young woman and a young child. Both child and Chesney had the same facial features smiling happily for the camera. There was no denying he fathered this child.

I had nobody to thank but Monty for being such a thorough and resourceful investigator. He's never disappointed me in the ten years that I've known him. Somehow, he was able to locate Chesney's secret love child with one of the former employees who was still on the payroll ten years after she left the company—I'd never ask how he was able to obtain such evidence nor I'd ever complain.

After my exhilarating call with Moffatt, I had to share this euphoria with someone much deserving. Moments later, Mrs. Chesney was on the line. She was satisfied with the update, and I promised to call her first moment should a settlement be reached.

Anything's possible, but losing this case was not; and if there's an out-of-court settlement according to the terms proposed, that would earn the firm $25 million and a hefty bonus for myself.

I was surprised that Monty called me late two nights ago asking me to represent his godson, Asa Payne, who was being held in a South Florida jail cell. I told him that I was licensed to practice in Florida, but that I would have to check my schedule to see what I could arrange.

So I had our firm's travel agent Tamala Dinkins schedule flights for Monty and myself. Within an hour, we had our itinerary and we were set to leave Charleston International on a 6:45 morning flight. We would change planes in Atlanta and then fly directly into Miami, landing about 10:20 a.m.

Laying eyes on Monty was pure pleasure. He's tall, lean, and muscular. His bald, sexy head reminded me of a chocolate Milk Dud that I did not mind it melted in my hands. For our trip, he was dressed for the mid-January weather wearing a navy pea coat and matching blue skull hat. The small diamond earring he wore in his left ear sparkled in the morning sunlight.

We had flirted in the past with one another; it was always in fun and in good taste. But if I were ever to mix business with pleasure, I could not imagine anything better than wrapping my legs around his sexy body.

Hey, I'm single and he's not married. No harm fantasizing, right?

On our ride to the airport, Monty caught me up to speed with the evidence that he'd gathered thus far—damn, this man's voice was so mesmerizing!

"These seem to be trumped up charges on Asa," he said. "In the early hours Tuesday morning, he was picked up for questioning about an armed robbery that took place while he visited friends for a Miami Heat basketball game."

Monty went on to describe that at the time of Asa's arrest, his rental car matched the description of the getaway car. He then reached into a folder.

"I managed to have copies made of the surveillance still shots of Asa at the game and another when he left the parking garage, all stamped with a date and time . . . And this is a copy of the receipt showing that Asa was at Hooter's, a couple of blocks away from the American Airlines Arena.

"When we land in Miami, I want to follow-up on Asa's waitress, Destiny. I want statements and any other employees who remember seeing Asa. When I called last night, one of the waitresses remembered Asa because they were flirting with each other the entire time he was there. She said she could confirm his alibi."

I chortled and glanced at him. "You don't need me; you've practically laid all the ground work. All I have to do is follow the dots."

Monty leaned back in the passenger's seat, exhaling. "Cole, you know how to get shit done. That's why I called you. Besides, no one can get access to the inmate except his attorney. Me bailing him out would only . . . well, complicate other matters."

I wasn't going to press him. I knew enough about Monty to know that he had jobs other than spying on cheating spouses.

"Like I said, I know who to go to if I want shit done right," he added, winking at me.

Immediately, I turned and looked straight ahead. I reminded myself once again that I wanted my success at the firm based on my merits and not by me laying on my back.

We took only carry-on baggage for this trip, so when we landed at Miami International Airport all we had to do was board the executive transportation services vehicle that awaited us at curbside.

Monty gave the driver the address to the restaurant where Destiny worked. She had already signed an affidavit attesting her encounter with Asa. In it, she stated that although it was busy on the night of the game, she distinctly remembered Asa because he commented on the tattoo of her astrology sign that he, too, was a Scorpio. He also gave her a twenty-five percent tip, which she really appreciated since she's a college student. She ended the interview recalling that Asa and his party left the restaurant a little after midnight.

Our interview with Destiny lasted thirty minutes. We hung around a little longer to see if there were other collaborators. Destiny mentioned that her co-worker, Saundra, was not scheduled until the weekend, but she would be willing to talk to us, if needed.

"In my opinion, Monty, Destiny is more than enough as a witness," I said. "She was observant, meticulous, witty, and intelligent."

"She seems to have her act together," he remarked. I'm not surprised that she did."

The next stop was the Miami-Dade County police. We were directed to the detective in charge of the case. My first impression of him was one of those arrogant ex-jock types being that he still maintained a muscular physique.

"I'm Detective Lambert," he said, extending his hand out towards me. "I understand you're representing someone who's been processed into our Metro West location?"

"Yes, I'm here for Asa Payne."

The detective offered us a seat in his modest office. The walls were dingy grey, but he proudly displayed all his accomplishments—a couple of awards from the city that recognized his dedication and courage. Not surprisingly, he was a family man. There were also a couple of pieces of child art inside picture frames.

"Detective, I'm still trying to understand why my client is in your custody." I adjusted my framed glasses and opened my attaché.

"According to the arrest report, your client apparently fit the description of a robbery suspect." He leaned back in his chair and folded his arms.

Since I was not one for wasting time, I pulled out the folder with all the information that Monty gathered. I handed Detective Lambert the still shots of Asa at the basketball game. I also provided him a copy of the restaurant receipt and Destiny's signed affidavit.

"I still don't know how you picked, of all people, my client," I said.

I noticed that Detective Lambert made a quick study of the evidence. I figured that I'd have to spend the better part of the day arguing and negotiating my client out of jail.

"All I can say is that the information that was provided to us was very credible. Given the location being Biscayne Bay and its clientele, it does not look good if we cannot provide a safe environment for patrons attending events in that area," he said. "That said, it's also obvious this is a case of mistaken identity."

"Okay, I'll take that," I replied. "I hope I'm not being too subtle. But I expect an expedited release, and that my client will be joining me on a flight back to Charleston in a few hours."

"I'll initiate the paperwork," he said. "And just to show that we made a mistake, hold on . . . ." He placed a call to the officer in charge at the facility requesting for Asa's immediate release. "Yes, that's right . . . ATW [all the way]. I anticipate that his attorney will be over there to receive him into her custody in about a forty-five minutes."

To say the least, the meeting went well. Monty was beaming, and he confided in me that he was impressed with my professionalism and no nonsense attitude. What he witnessed was merely the tip of the iceberg of what I do in a courtroom.

"I'll say this much, I overheard an adversary once refer to me as an 'Ice Queen.' It is true that I can be cold, calculating, and heartless."

Actually, I'm really a softy. I would like nothing better than to snuggle up to my man while eating bon bons and watching old movies. And Monty surely would be a desirable candidate.

Hey, I'm single and he's not married. No harm fantasizing, right?

"Hey, it takes all kinds," Monty quipped. "The challenge is always finding the right person for the job."

"But it was your work that gave me a leg to stand on."

Asa walked through the door a free man. Monty was first to get up and greet his godson. They gave each other a shoulder bump and a handshake.

I overheard Asa tell Monty, "I can't thank you enough for what you've done."

""It's all over and done with," Monty replied. "But the next time, I can't guarantee I will be there to pick up the pieces."

Then Monty turned and introduced Asa to me. He was just as tall as Monty, standing about six-two. He appeared to be in his mid-twenties. He was clean cut and light skinned with hazel eyes. His tattoos were not obvious. He spoke with good diction. He was opposite of what I expected for somebody his age.

"Ms. Kennedy, thank you so much for believing me."

"You're welcome, but the thanks goes to your godfather."

There was a diner not far from the facility, and we decided to go there to eat before we headed back to the airport. I sat directly across from Asa, and I studied him while he and Monty conversed.

"Were you treated well?" Monty asked.

Asa shrugged his shoulders. "Yeah, I guess. I mean, nobody ever messed with me. It's definitely not a place I want to see again."

"Do you have any idea why you were profiled?"

"No. None." He paused and took a sip of water from his glass. "All I can say is that me and a couple of friends had just left the Hooters on Biscayne Boulevard. I was getting into my rental car when two plain clothes officers, with their guns drawn, told me to put my hands on the hood of the car and do not move.

"When I asked, 'what did I do?' They told me that I fit the description of an armed robbery suspect."

Monty nodded then shook his head.

"The only thing that I could think of was that whoever was their robbery suspect was twenty-something and black," Asa continued.

"How many times I've told you about being a young black male?" Monty queried; he sat back with his arms folded.

Asa snorted loudly. "Countless of times. I can tell people first-hand about it now." He also bunched his thin, succulent lips before he spoke. "I kept telling them they were making a mistake. All they kept telling me was it was their job to sort it all out."

"Well, that was similar to what they told us, if that's of any consolation," I chimed in to say. "I'm glad that things worked out in your favor."

The waitress had now come by with our orders. It was apparent that Asa did not take too well to the jail's food as he quickly downed three pancakes and the bacon and eggs. He had also drunk two full glasses of soda. He looked like he could have had another order.

I mentioned to Asa that the legal system does work, but so much is involved.

"Oh, I forgot to mention that while they were insistent that they had the right person, I heard before I was released that the Feds were wanting to talk to me. They wanted to know about my relationship with some a local proprietor named Diego Fonseca-Garbey.

"That's when I knew something was really wrong, so I decided to call the only person I knew who could help me — Monty."

I looked over at Monty. He was so full of himself. He knew his shit was tight, and it took all of him not to puff out his chest in sheer pride.

Just then, Monty's phone went off and he excused himself to answer it. Leaving Asa alone with me worked out fine.

"Please call my assistant Jabree tomorrow. I'll have a few questions I need to go over with you in case any federal agents need to interrogate you."

I handed him my business card, which he eagerly accepted and placed in his wallet.

By four o'clock, Asa and I were on our way to Miami International. Monty said he would be in Miami a little longer than expected. I understood what that meant. The man does more than just spy on cheating spouses.

Chapter 26

Asa Payne

Miami, Florida

I was escorted back to my cell block by one of the correctional officers whose name badge had GRANT on it. It was as if he was an animal trainer and I was the caged animal with him following me as I walked along the right side of a jail corridor. I was property of the Miami-Dade County jail system.

"Look straight ahead and be quiet," Grant told me; I also overheard him behind me making quick and light conversation with another inmate who had just passed by us.

We passed through another set of doors. I could never get used to the loud buzzing and clicking followed by them shutting like a bank's vault.

While waiting for what seemed to be the last series of doors to open, Grant spoke to me in a serious tone. It was different than the loud and jovial tenor that I had become accustomed to.

"What you got yourself into, anyway?" he inquired.

"Some bullshit that I robbed a liquor store, "I answered. "I've been trying to tell anyone who would listen to me that I was at a Miami Heat basketball game."

"Liquor store?" he reacted; his Florida dialect was different than what I'd become familiar with in South Carolina. "Naw, man. Not you—"

After returning to my cell block, I sat off to myself, replaying in my head everything that had transpired thus far. It was as if I had been singled out by the cops, but I still did not know why.

It could not be because of a robbery, I surmised. Other than being a male, I could not imagine anything else about the individual being like me. Something was not right.

About thirty minutes later, everyone was ordered back on lockdown. A couple of boneheads had gotten into an argument, so the correctional officers had everyone to get back into their cells, where there were two inmates to each holding space, until further notice.

I should have known better.

The command for lights out occurred around 11:00 p.m. I remembered Grant telling everyone once lights are out they do not come back on until 5 a.m. Then breakfast is served around 5:30 a.m.

I had about fallen asleep when the speaker went off in my cell.

"Payne, I need you to step outside your cell." The door clicked open. Standing just outside was Grant, who told me to place my hands against the wall and spread my feet apart. I found it annoying that he would be frisking me down and inspecting whether I had any weapons on me. Hell, I had everything taken from me and before I was placed in a cell.

"Hey, I'm talking about the Feds are coming to see you tomorrow," Grant whispered to me.

I did not bother to look back at him because I did not want to draw any attention to us. "The Feds? Why would they be coming to see me?"

"I don't know, but watch your back." Grant then told me to go back inside my cell. I overheard him going to another cell, requesting for another person to come outside.

I wondered whether Grant knew what in the hell he was talking about, nor did I really know what to think. Perhaps he had confused me with another inmate. The more I thought about it, the more I suspected that I may have been set up all along.

* * *

The morning could not come any sooner. I knew that I needed to do something. But I could not do it until we were not under lockdown.

The first chance I got, I dialed collect to a familiar number—someone whom I held in the highest of esteem.

"Monty, I'm so glad that I finally caught you."

"You're lucky. That's all I'll say," he replied, having answered on the second ring.

"I need your help."

"I can tell by the phone number something must be wrong. You're in Florida. What's going on?"

I began telling Monty the course of events that led me to this fucking place. I also told him how the Feds are supposed to visit with me this morning.

"Monty, I swear. I just came out to see a basketball game. They have the wrong man." I wanted to cry, but I was not going to let these Florida motherfuckers think that I got punk running through my Charleston, South Carolina veins.

"I hope this shit don't become a habit of yours," Monty grumbled. "I don't want to hear or see that you're doing shit you ain't supposed to. 'Cause if your mother—"

"Monty, it's not like that. I swear on Pops' grave. I'm innocent," I interrupted him; I heard a system voice telling me that I had one minute remaining on my call.

"Why don't you try calling me back in an hour? By then, I'll have more information to work off of. Just tell me where you're at right now."

"Miami-Dade County Jail . . ."

The phone call terminated right after I got out those last syllables. I did feel much better knowing if there was anyone who could get me out of this shit, it was Monty.

There were two phones in the cell block, but only one of them worked. And that one was being held up by an inmate who had called his girlfriend, talking as if they were neighbors out in the back yard having a barbecue.

"Yeah, I can't wait to get out 'cause I'm gonna bang you from here to Bangkok," he said, laughing.

Now this was some bullshit. But there were two other people ahead of me. They had even less patience.

"Motherfucker, take that shit somewhere else. Like if and when you get your ass outta here!" one snarled.

"You just wait your damn turn!"

The best thing that happened was one of the correctional officers came by and ordered him off the phone. "This is a jail, and not some damn country club."

I waited another ten minutes before I got my chance to call again. I prayed that Monty would still be waiting.

He answered on the first ring.

"What took you so damn long?" he asked.

"Monty—"

"All right, all right. I'll cut you some slack."

I breathed another sigh of relief.

"I caught up with my contact in Florida . . . hold on," he said, pausing. "Okay, here's the deal. You'll be out tomorrow. Me and attorney Cole Kennedy will be there tomorrow. Just hang in there."

Monty then hung up. I never got a chance to tell him about the Feds wanting to speak with me. I still had no idea what they wanted nor did I really care. I set my heart and sights on walking out of this place.

The FBI came just as Grant said wanting to interview me. I did not mind talking to them because it was a chance not to sit in a fucking jail cell. The inmate that was there when I arrived had made bail, so I was alone for a while. I'd become so bored that I counted squares and figured out that my cell was about twelve feet by nine feet. Not much room to do much of anything.

"Do you know why we're talking to you?" one of the agents asked.

"No, not really."

"So we have a smart ass, don't we?"

"I wouldn't say that. You asked me a question, and I answered it."

"Okay, well tell me what dealings do you have with local businessman Diego Fonseca-Garbey?" he said.

"I'm a club promoter. I have dealings with a lot of club owners. But I was here only for a basketball game."

"Are you aware of any other of his business interests?"

I shook my head. "I book acts to his clubs, and that's the extent of our relationship. What I do is credible. I'm sure you can access my tax returns."

It was apparent that neither of these FBI agents were buying my story. I could care less because if they had anything concrete they would not just be questioning my relationships with businessmen.

Besides, I suspect that I would have been in some kind of federal detention center.

"And where you say you're from?" the agent asked; it was obvious he was trying to test me for any inconsistencies.

"I already told you that I'm from South Carolina."

"Where in South Carolina?"

"Charleston."

The agent had a look of smugness, bordering sarcasm. "If you're from Charleston, what business do you have here in South Florida?"

I broke out laughing. "That's what I've been trying to tell all of you. I was here to see a basketball game." I knew that I must have pissed him off, but what could he do?

The agent looked to his left beyond my shoulder and nodded. He told me that I could leave. I was escorted back to my cell block. But I was not there long this time.

"Asa Payne!" a female corrections officer yelled.

"Yeah, I'm Asa Payne."

I got up from the chair that I was sitting in near a doorway entry into a miniature yard and walked towards her desk. However, inmates could not walk beyond the red line that bordered the correctional officer's area.

"Get all of your stuff and come with me."

"What for?"

"You're ATW."

"What's that?"

"All the way; you're leaving."

The best thing I'd seen in nearly three days was Monty and the woman that accompanied him. I immediately sensed that she was my attorney, Ms. Kennedy. It was hard not looking into her eyes because she reminded me of my girlfriend, Natana.

Her designer purple rectangular-framed glasses matched her suit perfectly.

"I'm so glad to be out of here," I exclaimed; I did not bother to look behind me because I wanted no final memories of that fucking jail.

I gave Monty a hug and we bumped fists. After we chatted a bit, Ms. Kennedy spoke up.

"Whatever reason they had you here was purely circumstantial," she said.

Then she suggested that we go to a restaurant. Our plane would be leaving later this afternoon.

At the restaurant, I told Ms. Kennedy about the FBI questioning me about Diego Garbey. I was surprised at myself that I even recalled it considering how hungry I was.

There was nothing in that fucking jail worth eating or drinking. I had never been so appreciative of a fresh, hot meal in my life.

"You may be considered a person of interest, but I wouldn't worry about that. I think the people around here will back off you and concentrate on finding the real assailant or assailants," Ms. Kennedy said.

"I warned the detective if he so much as insinuate you were involved in any robbery that I would slap the Miami-Dade Police Department so hard with a discrimination and harassment lawsuit, and so fast, that they would be tasting blood for a week."

This woman had composure. I knew that I was in good hands along with Monty.

"I love how you think," I said. "And I really appreciate you coming here to help on such short notice. I don't know what I would have been facing without your help."

Taking out her pen and pad, she replied, "You can thank your lucky stars later. We need to go over why the FBI is so interested in you."

Chapter 27

Stefan Lewis
Los Angeles, California

Yeah, whatever!

"Breakfast in ten minutes." Brother Clayton yelled from the other side of the door.

Why do they have to bother me every goddamn morning with the same shit?

I know I need to be up and dressed by 7 a.m. if I want hot breakfast. And I have to be out the door by eight to start my mundane day of searching for gainful employment, as a part of my probation to stay at this half-way house.

What a routine. Mondays and Wednesdays I comb the streets of Los Angeles searching for a job. It's been fruitless. Not many places seem willing to take a chance on a crazy ex-criminal—that's what the legal system says I am. The other days of the week are spent in revivals, meetings, and spiritual counseling. For the most part, the staff has been pleasant, but I've become tired of these hypocrites dictating my life.

My life belongs with Cole, and my being another day without her is killing me to the core. I know in my heart that she's missed me much in the way I've missed her. I've just wanted to be there for her.

"Brother Lewis, don't forget you have an eight o'clock session with Pastor Troy," Brother Clayton yelled again.

Yeah, whatever!

Forcing me to participate in their program of faith, love, and bullshit.

Besides, how can I ever forget my counseling sessions with the infamous Pastor Troy Aiken and his less-than-Christian-based program? I have been here for eleven months, and I could write a juicy gossip column or book on the stories of sex and drugs that have occurred here.

"Brother Lewis . . ." Brother Clayton yelled, knocking on the door a little harder.

"I didn't forget. I'll be out in a second," I answered, forcing myself to sound as cheery as he.

Brother Clayton mumbled something I could not understand; the floor beneath him creaked as he walked to the next room and lightly knocked on the door. He's a good man, but his annoying habit of bothering me when I don't feel like socializing simply irks the hell out of me.

Instead of prison, I was assigned to the state's mental health facility in Vacaville, and they kept me there for ten years. I was primarily diagnosed as being bipolar and schizophrenic, and the psychiatrist noted in my charts that I had also developed erotomaniac delusions that stemmed from a distorted reality regarding my relationship with Cole. He thought I had a weird fixation on Cole, whom he said was never my fiancée.

Humph, I knew the "truth" no matter what any other person said.

How would they know anything about my relationship with Cole? What they obviously didn't know is how real love was supposed to look and function. I was livid they thought my relationship with Cole was a figment of my imagination.

Cole and I had a real relationship, damnit. We were about to be married until I was wrongly convicted of the attempted murder of Jamil Holdings and the murder of Barry Kinloch.

Regardless of how they put it, I helped society by ridding it of criminals and it repaid me by sending me to some nut house in the middle of fucking nowhere.

I should have been rewarded with an outstanding citizens' award for taking the initiative to clean the community by ridding it of thugs and criminals.

"Brother Lewis, it's time for your session," Pastor Troy greeted me as I entered his office.

Yeah, whatever!

* * *

Initially, I was upset that Cole never visited me inside the hospital. Then it occurred to me that she could not bear to see me in that state being locked up like some caged animal. It probably would have driven her insane seeing me. She probably would have tried to commit herself so that she could be next to me. I could not let her ruin her life over a careless mistake.

So, I did not blame her for not seeing me. She had a lot on her mind. She had to focus on her law career. Being strong and trying to survive this cold world without her protective shield would have been hard for her, especially for someone who lost everything the way she did.

Being at a looney bin facility showed me that there were really a lot of crazy motherfuckers that walked the streets. I had to deal with those crazies inside and the so-called normal people that supposedly took care of us crazy people.

Over time, Cole did write me a few letters, although they never had any return addresses on them. I wished that I had the chance to express my gratitude. With nothing else to do, I went as far as memorizing each word that was written to me. Over time, Cole did write me a few letters, although they never had any return addresses on them. I wished that I had the chance to express my gratitude. With nothing else to do, I went as far as memorizing each word that was written to me.

My Friend and Protector,

I am so appreciative of what you did in my life. I apologize for being so upset when you last saw me. When I finally had a chance to think about it, it was such a turn-on. Now I wished that I had a chance to express the way I felt. Stay strong for me!

Love,

Cole

That's right. These people had no idea how love really functioned. Then there's the letter that kept me focused the most while I was locked up among societies deranged. I truly felt Cole's spirit and passion for our relationship.

She wrote,

Stefan, I could not believe the way I felt after the first time that our eyes ever met. I wish you were here with me right now. I hate having to pleasure myself, but I have no choice. Just know you're in my heart and mind as I try and keep my sanity for another day.

But then the letters stopped coming after that one. While I clung on to those thoughts she conveyed to me, I soon realized that she was heartbroken just as I was and she could not endure the separation.

I understood. It didn't matter what others thought. We were meant to be together. They never understood our bond and special love for one another.

So I say fuck 'em!

I do believe that love endures all things, although my mother has told me to let her go.

She argued, "How much time has passed without even a letter should tell you that Cole has moved on."

"Mother, I can't. I won't."

Then we got into an argument over my lame ass father. I told her that I've had absolutely no respect for the man.

"If I ever see his punk ass, I'm going to beat him down as if he'd stolen something," I said. "How can I respect him, and I was the result of a rape?"

"Stefan, there's too much rage built inside you. You can't live the rest of your life hating, or not letting go."

She tried to reason with me, but this was the same person who forgot to love me as her child. Whenever she looked in my eyes, she, too, saw nothing but hate.

"I don't understand how you can go around preaching that to me," I said. "You sound about as bad as those people in that facility in the middle of nowhere. Why didn't you ever hate that sorry bastard you said was my father?"

I knew that I had cut right to her heart, so I went for twisting and jiggling it inside.

"Why did you send me off to your parents? You left me. You walked away and never looked back—until now. And now you want to tell me that I need to let Cole go?"

She appeared as if she wanted to slap me. I looked at her, daring her to do it.

"Do you know what it felt like carrying a child created through violence? Too embarrassed. Ashamed. Then looking into that child's eyes only to see the monster that degraded me. Took my innocence and left me to die."

She began crying.

Yeah, whatever!

"Your blood runs through my veins, too," I retorted. "I did not ask to be here. You chose not to abort. You had to have felt something for me."

That was the last time we'd spoken to each other.

I plan on stopping by the city library after my session with Pastor Troy. I've got some researching to do. It's cool that these places have computers and Internet access. There was no such thing like that while I was in Seattle and before my run-in with the law here in California.

Perhaps I could find Cole on the social network or dating websites, but I've not had much luck so far. How can someone just vanish from the face of the earth?

I never knew any of her friends other than Sydney, but I've since learned that she's been missing in action since her involvement in a prostitution ring. The Internet's a cool thing. I even learned that happened to her nearly five years ago.

Chapter 28

Sydney Starks
Inglewood, California

I left a message with Cole's legal assistant to call me no matter how late it was. It was urgent that I spoke to her. I just hope she's not too busy to return my call.

Since I've been receiving anonymous messages about "The Cyclone" Waters, I wanted to know if she's been receiving them, too. She was there as well, so why would I be singled out?

If its ransom they want, I can't help them. The prison conviction bankrupted me. Why else would I be living back home with my mother and sleeping in the same bedroom as my sixteen-year-old sister?

I had done some research on Cole, and it seemed that life turned out great for her. She's a lawyer at a large firm in the South with a man as her assistant. It's still hard to imagine that, but she was always in the company of a man.

Too bad for her that she and Kavion broke up the way they did. She would have been living high off the hog. He went on to play professional football after he graduated from UCLA.

My own life path did not turn out the way I dreamt it would. I did not think my lucrative business would rise and fall in only five years.

For five years, I had it all. And with a drop of a hat, I lost everything—my apartment, car, and my money—because my business partner Reggie made questionable decisions that had Caramella Girl operating more like a prostitution ring than a true escort service.

Call it guilt by association. It also did not help that I was the "face" of the business. I served fifty-four months at Central California Women's Facility in Chowchilla, plus five years' probation, for it while he never stopped being in the business of prostitution.

After my release, I had nowhere to go, and I was forced to move back home with my mother Miranda and sisters, Londyn and Brooklyn.

It's been humiliating sleeping in the same room with my baby sister Brooklyn. My mother already told me how she found a boy hiding in the closet at one o'clock in the morning. So now I've had to sleep with one eye open just in case someone's being sneaked in at night.

It was inevitable that Brooklyn might turn out the way she has. I love my mother, but she's far from being one. She's never possessed any true maternal instinct.

Early on, she required us to call her Miranda because she did not want the men she dated to know she had three kids. I don't know if she bought into her own lies because she paraded around town as if she had no responsibilities at home.

She would rather snort a line than go to a parent's night for any of us. I was the one who would prepare my sisters' breakfast, dress them, and made sure their hair was combed for school. When the school needed someone to pick up my sisters, I was the one they called. And while my mother often slept in a comatose state, too fucked up on coke or whatever the choice of drug of the night she was privy to, I learned quickly never to fuck with her whenever she did not want to be bothered. Because it would have been met with a slap, punch, or knock to the head.

The comatose state that I often found her in was from her being a stripper. For as long as I could remember, she and her stripper friends would spend all evening practicing their routines. Their partying started hours before they actually went out with all the snorting, popping of pills, and drinking.

They used to think it was cute that my little sisters and I would imitate their raunchy moves, gyrating our hips and humping the walls.

"Miranda, you better watch your back. Sydney will be stealing your customers in a few years," Starr, a stripper friend of my mother laughed as she applied her makeup on the makeshift vanity table.

"That bitch can't do it like I can," my mother retorted, while she gave her ass to kiss before dropping it to the floor.

Her crooked smile faded as she slapped the floor with her ass. I knew she was high. I just never knew what type of mood she was in—happy, bitchy, or abusive; most times it was the latter. It would have been a total shock if she were not high.

I remembered that night because Starr stared at me with pity in her eyes, but then she chastised my mother for referring to me as a bitch.

"I remember how mad you got a couple of nights ago when that belligerent asshole called you all kinds of bitches. You damn near knocked his head off. So why would you call your own daughters that name?"

Starr reached into her diamond-like studded bra and pulled out two crisp ten dollar bills. She handed the money to my sister and me, told us to go across the street to Mickey D's, and treat ourselves to dinner before they left for their show. We thought we were like royalty that night because we got to order whatever we wanted.

Because of the example in our lives, Brooklyn's being into boys was to be expected. But if she doesn't slow down, she might end up like Londyn with a baby and a deadbeat ass for a boyfriend living in her bedroom without any job to support himself or concern how his baby eats.

The sound of the cell phone vibration interrupted my miserable, pathetic self-rant. I glanced at the number. Anxiety rose as I recognized the 843 area code. I answered before the call went into voice mail.

"Hello, Sydney, is everything all right?" Cole had asked before I had a chance to get in my hellos. She sounded as though we never lost touch.

I started to say yes, but I felt I needed to tell her the truth. So I spent the next hour catching her up on the latest tales of my life. I also told her how I got arrested.

"If I ever catch up to Reggie, I'm going to break every fucking bone in his body," I said. "He's the reason why I lost everything. That pimp streak in his ass got too big and wide, and as soon as they started applying pressure to his ass he sung like a fucking sissy in a church choir."

I explained to Cole that Reggie copped a plea bargain and got six months in exchange for having me arrested as the brains behind everything.

"And the bad thing about it, his ass still ran a prostitution ring while he was in prison. Now he's got layers of people protecting his ass. But if I ever catch up to him . . ."

"I think you know that I never cared much for your former business partner," Cole said.

"Well, I don't think much of that motherfucker. He's a dead bitch ass in my book."

Thoughts of prison had my blood pressure about to spike. I decided not to share with Cole how I had to fight for respect damn near every day that I was there, or I might have been turned out as somebody's bitch.

The only thing that kept me going was reminding myself that I was a college graduate, and eventually I'd be able to turn my life around some way, somehow. It still hasn't. Not many have wanted to take a chance. And if they've been willing, there's been a catch to it.

Shit, I might as well get into porn. At least it would be somewhat legal; they are supposed to pay taxes.

"Cole, this is the real reason why I called you. I need to know if you've been getting any strange messages lately."

"What are you talking about?"

"Somebody has been dropping hints about The Cyclone—you do remember him?"

The conversation became quiet.

"I don't know anything about that. What type of messages you're talking about?"

"They know what I did and they said I deserved what I got. I was assuming they were referring to my conviction. That was until they mentioned Malibu the last time they left one," I said. "Whoever it is, they're barking up the wrong tree if its money they want."

"Do this for me," Cole said. "Forward me the messages. I'll look into it. Meanwhile, don't respond to them. And do not under any circumstance give them what they ask for—"

"Girl, in case you weren't listening, I'm staying with my mother and sisters."

"I understand. But you know, once you start they will only ask for more. Here's what I'm going to do. I'll call you back in the middle of the week. I hope to have a few more details and a strategy to share with you."

Chapter 29

Cole Kennedy
Charleston, South Carolina

Damn!

I did the ultimate no-no in my rule book—or anybody's for that matter.

I made a booty call to one of my exes because I felt horny after a few of my friends and I went out for drinks. All night we talked about sex.

Yeah, Cole, you look like the freaky type.

Girl, lemme tell you. I'll always suck me some dick. You gotta get his attention the best way you can . . .

Uh-huh, but if I put my lips on any dick, the favor's gotta be returned. Head first, you know what I mean? He's gotta eat some of this pussy. Cole, you know what I'm talkin' about!

All of you are crazy.

I'm not crazy. That's just the way it is.

Yeah, girl, I can't tell him every time that he's hitting my spot or that shit will definitely go to his head. But that shit be feeling good!

214 | J Lynn

I had no one to go home to, and I did not want to resort to mechanical means of dealing with my need for some stress-relieving sex.

I felt that I had deserved it after all the hard work that I had put in at the law firm lately. So, I went backwards and contacted Teague. We had broken up—again—a couple of months ago because he could not keep his dick inside his pants. But he's been the only one that could make my toes curl.

"Bueno?"

"Don't give me that Dominican shit," I answered playfully. "What are you doing?"

"Who is this?"

"So now you're going to act like you have amnesia?"

"Cole?"

"Yes, it is."

"Oh, hey." There was some uncertainty still in his voice. "I can't believe that you're calling me. What did I do to deserve this honor?"

"Nothing. Actually, I was talking to some friends of mine and I thought about you."

"Really?" he answered, chortling.

"Yes, really. So, what are you doing right now?"

"Well, nothing."

"Nothing? You, the hot-blooded Latino who can't keep his dick inside his pants is actually doing nothing right now. What happened?"

"You would go there, wouldn't you—?"

"Teague, I only speak to you at the firm when I have to. I don't know what else is going on in your personal life. Obviously, something's happened."

"I really don't want to talk about it."

I sensed there was some hurt in his voice. I found it unusual because he had been the one responsible for the other person's hurt, including mine. But this was about me, and me only.

"You sound like you could use some company," I posed to him, as I counted on him never being the type to refuse a good piece of ass.

Sighing, he replied, "I'm surprised that you called. But I thought you were finished with me after what happened the last time. I keep telling you that I was the one who wasn't chasing, but you never believed me."

The lilt in his accent had me thinking about the times when he would talk me out of my panties and he would fill my passion with his. And the throbbing between my thighs drove home that moment of reflection.

"All right, let's do this. I'll forgive and forget this last time."

"You would, uh, you will?" he reacted.

"Sure, as long as it can be mutually beneficial—"

I rang his doorbell and after a few moments, he opened the door. Even if I'd thought about turning back, seeing him in his robe and small amount of curly chest hair peeking out, I knew I could not resist my Latin lover.

We did not speak. As soon as I entered his home, he led me to his bedroom. It had not changed since we last were hot and sweaty under the bed sheets.

Undressing me until I was wearing only my thong, he pushed me onto his queen-size bed and pounced atop me. We kissed and rubbed against each other. The room was full of our moans. It had me wondering why I allowed him to slip through my fingers, but I could not have a meaningful relationship with such a whore.

"You're so sexy," he whispered to me.

I did not respond verbally. Instead, I returned the favor and flipped him over, allowing him to rest on his back. Sensually, I caressed his dick and balls until he was deliciously at my mercy. It was as if he begged me to do more.

Thus, I proceeded to lick and suck his dick until I tasted the sweet cum that was forming. I gave a loud smack and kissed the head. I nudged him to spread his legs before I proceeded to straddle him.

"How do you want me?" I asked.

He rose from the bed and flipped me around to one of my favorite positions: face down, ass up; doggie style.

I propped my right leg on the foot of the bed, spread my ass cheeks wide, and waited for his entry. He smiled and licked his lips just as he bent forward and pushed his tongue inside my pussy.

"Mmm, that's it," I hissed, while I pushed my ass into his face. "That's it. Lick that pussy!"

Just as I was about to release, he withdrew only to return with his dick, easing strokes inside my steamy flesh. We had not yet gotten into a fast rhythm before I felt the first orgasmic wave ripple throughout my body. It was exactly what I wanted—and needed from him.

He was a master at fucking, and I was content with giving him something that I could also feel that night.

Although guilt came upon me no sooner than our moment ended, I was quick at reasoning to myself that I got mine; he got his and I was under no obligation to thank him for it.

That's exactly what a booty call is, right?

Chapter 30

Stefan Lewis
Los Angeles, California

I found her!

I could not believe all the hard work had finally paid off. There was an article written about Cole on Forbes.com, and it talked about her recent multi-million dollar win against a big corporate boss. Now she's the youngest partner in her practice.

There was another article where she and thirty-nine other honorees were this year's most notable professionals under the age of forty. There would be a gala in three weeks to celebrate her and the other candidate's accomplishments.

This would be perfect. My probation will be over in a week, and I would be free to accompany her in honor of her impressive achievements.

I began surfing the Internet for airline prices and found a one-way ticket to Charleston International for seven hundred and fifty dollars. I didn't care how much it cost or how far I had to go to be with her, just as long she was near me. As long as we're reunited nothing else mattered.

I've been so eager to wrap my arms around her and give what she's been missing for ten years.

When I told mother, she was pleased that Cole and I were a couple again.

"Mother, I need you to wire me some money to hold me over until I could get on my feet." I asked, knowing she would give me whatever I wanted.

She married into wealth, so money was never an issue. I told her that I found a reasonable room for rent that was within my budget.

"Stefan, I'm not getting any younger. All my girlfriends show me pictures of their grandchildren and all I have is a picture of Snookie, my cat," she complained.

"Cole and I are getting married first," I retorted. "We agreed that we would wait until our careers and our lives together are stable before we bring kids into the equation."

"Stefan, you know I worry about you so much; you need to settle down have kids and live a normal life."

Yeah, whatever!

And this was coming from my mother who can be such a drama queen—and a nag.

"While I'm at it, no more of this getting in trouble with the law. First, there was the incident with Brady. Then this attempted murder and you being sent off to a psychiatric facility; your grandmother didn't raise you this way."

She's always harassed me about the way I've lived my life. As if every aspect revolved around her. Then blaming herself when shit hit the fan.

This is the same woman who walked in on me having sex with a neighbor's daughter when I was fifteen. The girl later cried rape, which was all lies. I was finally exonerated after we threatened to sue her family for slander.

Then there was the incident at the college I attended before Washington State. I was investigated for being a peeping Tom. She almost had a heart attack. Admittedly, I did see a lady who lived in the neighborhood having sex with men who visited her. I always found it so amusing how she thought she had the greatest moves in bed—what was so great about fucking in the missionary position and each man having premature ejaculation?

Fortunately, I worked out an agreement with her that I would not tell anyone about her whoring around in exchange for her dropping the charges—with a little help from my stepfather's bank account and my doing what those men couldn't do for her.

There was also my last encounter with the law and the resulting wrongful conviction. Although I've always claimed my innocence, my mother always blamed herself.

"Tomas and I think it would be best if you—"

"If I what?"

"If you had a father figure in your life, you would have been normal."

Yeah, whatever!

She thought marrying a wealthy jackass would compensate for the lack of a father figure. Although Tomas paid for my education, he spoke to me as if I was a heathen.

"Mother, can't we just talk about me being happy for a change?"

"Well, I'm glad if you and Cole have decided to give it a try," she said. "So, when am I going to meet her?"

"Before the wedding, of course, mother. It will be soon, I promise. Maybe we could fly up for the holidays."

I figured that she would let it go since that was something she missed about that time of the year. Before my grandfather passed away, my grandmother's home was the main gathering place. It was also where she sent me to stay part of my childhood.

Once she got married, she would invite me to Tomas' family ranch to spend a couple of days with his family riding horses and canoeing on the lake.

I wonder what would be different this time if and when me and Cole showed up.

Oh, well.

By the time I hung up the phone, my mother was excited about meeting her future daughter-in-law. The proof was in her wiring me seven thousand dollars, which was enough for me to get on my feet and concentrate on finding a job and making a living for Cole and myself.

Once I'm gainfully employed again, she could stop pestering me about giving her grand kids.

"Don't expect that to happen immediately. But it will happen. Cole and I are working on our careers first so we might have time to raise our children the right way," I reminded her.

"Stefan, I'm not getting any younger, in case you've forgotten. Sometimes, you do have a short memory span."

"Mother, after we're married I promise I'll make you the doting grandmother you've always wanted to be."

Although I don't believe there would be a problem staying at Cole's place, I did not want to impose. We would have the rest of our lives to live together. Surely, we'd be taking it one day at a time.

I even shared the good news with my housemates at the halfway house that I was soon to be reunited with my girlfriend, and that we were planning to be married.

Everyone was excited for me. They even sent me off with a party on my last day of fulfilling my terms of probation. I was so excited about being on my way to South Carolina to be with my lover.

Chapter 31

Cole Kennedy
Charleston, South Carolina

It was only six months ago when I won the Chesney case, a huge divorce settlement resulted in my client earning $75 million dollars from her cheating husband. But these last six months have also been so draining. I've never worked so hard before. The time has surely flown by so fast—it's especially fun when a lot of money's being made.

I'd only stopped in the office to wrap up a few loose ends before I took my week-long sabbatical to the Caribbean. I'd been in there only a few moments when my phone began buzzing—I knew that Jabree was not at his desk.

"Ms. Kennedy—"

Shit!

It was the receptionist downstairs, Phoebe Reynolds. Her high-pitched voice always annoyed the hell out of me. She's twenty-two. But whenever she opened her mouth, she sounded like a whiny four-year-old child.

"There is a visitor here to see you." She paused; there was unrecognizable chatter between her and a male visitor.

Then she shrieked like she was some silly high school groupie. After several seconds of silence, I sighed loudly.

"Well, are you going to tell me who it is, or am I going to have to read your mind?" I'm sure she sensed the displeasure in my voice, but I tried reminding myself that she would be returning to college in a month.

"Uh, sorry, Ms. Kennedy. The gentleman that is here . . . I can't believe I'm speaking to Mr. Kavion Cottrell," she shrieked again into the phone.

My Kavion, here and unannounced? I thought to myself.

"Ms. Kennedy, why didn't you tell me you know Mr. Cottrell? Can I get your autograph?"

"Phoebe, tell Mr. Cottrell I will be down in a couple of minutes. Please try to keep it professional. This is a law firm and not some meat market," I advised before I hung up.

I shook my head in amazement. The child had no etiquette, but I guess being the daughter of one of the partners had its benefits—it's still a good thing she's leaving in a month.

I walked over to my private bathroom. Nothing extravagant, just a basin, a toilet, and a large vanity; I lucked up inheriting this corner office overlooking the Charleston harbor. It still doesn't compare to a couple of the major players in the firm. Their offices are equipped with showers, fireplaces, bars, and a small kitchenette.

I reapplied my lipstick and smoothed my hair in place. I cleared my desk of this Payne case that has consumed so much of my time, and I walked nervously out of my office.

Why on earth would Kavion be here after all this time? I wondered.

It had been more than ten years since I last seen or spoken to Kavion. That was just after I'd graduated from UCLA and I told him that I had accepted a job offer here in South Carolina. Thinking about him reminded me of my past: the pain, humiliation, and terror from being stalked that all stemmed from my rape case.

I had resolved when I left California that I would never look back—I can't believe that I actually forgotten about Stefan Lewis, and for ten years I did just that.

Being here in Charleston also reminded me of all these years of grinding, busting my ass and the many nights spent alone with only B.O.B., which gave me a few moments of gratification, had paid off.

I checked the mirrored elevator doors and made sure there was no smeared lipstick on my teeth before I exited. I entered the main lobby, its rich colors of African mahogany wood and cream marble tile that went half way up the walls. The two-story high ceiling held eight blown glass art that illuminated abstract bright water paint colors. Breathtaking. Amazing. The $45,000 large round crystal chandelier gave the reception area a comforting and relaxed feel.

I turned the corner and spotted Kavion in the sitting area. He sat with his legs outstretched looking like a tall, smooth glass of lemonade that could quench my body's thirst for male attention. He looked even better with a little age.

Our eyes met the moment he glanced beyond the edge of the USA Today that he'd been reading. He stood up quickly, beaming.

"Cole, you look stunning. I could have never thought of you looking even better," he said, giving me a warm hug.

I could not believe how much I had missed having Kavion's strong arms around my body. He stirred something in me, and it made me hot between my thighs.

Inwardly, I struggled to pull away amid what I felt was a dozen eyes burning a hole in the back of my skull.

"You haven't lost your way around a compliment," I replied. "I can't believe it. Ten years. Ten long years. What brings you here?"

I made a head-nod gesture that he followed me back up to my office. Once we reached the elevator, I extended my hand out for him to hold while I accompanied him there.

Even my nipples became sensitive and erect.

"This is awesome," Kavion exclaimed once we reached my office.

He then veered towards the wall where all my degrees and awards were hung. He took time to read each framed piece of recognition.

Meanwhile, I had sat down in my executive chair and reflected on the enormity of the moment. Being a firm believer in Feng Shui, I made sure the designer brought the five elements into my office, balancing the harmony and energy of success.

"And you've done all of this?" he asked.

"Yes, you might say that I have."

Kavion sat across from me in one of my mauve and tan striped guest chairs. "I guess you want to know why I'm here."

I nodded.

"A couple of teammates of mine and myself are in town for a benefit golf tournament. We're raising money for a football camp for underprivileged youths."

"I heard of the program. It does not surprise me that you would be involved in programs such as this. You always spent your extra time mentoring young boys at the YMCA" I smiled at the image of Kavion teaching his son how to ride a bike or throw a ball.

He smiled. "You remember all that?"

"I actually do."

I could not shake the images of our past rendezvous. I wondered if he had gotten better with age even there. I know I could show him a few new tricks or two. A devilish smiled crept over my face. I hoped he might know what thoughts I'd been entertaining and what I might be willing to accommodate with him.

Apparently, he had another agenda. His face turned serious. He sat back in the seat and folded his arms. "There is another reason why I'm here, Cole, and I need to ask a favor from you." He spoke calmly and I waited for him to continue.

"I saw you last night on television. I'm really proud of you and the way your career has turned out." His words seemed genuine; his eyes were locked in on mine. "But one of my teammates is involved in a paternity suit. The mother claims my friend was in Tennessee around the time this child was conceived, but I know for a fact that we were in Hawaii to play in the Pro Bowl and we stayed there for another week before we returned stateside."

He summed up the story that the petitioner also claimed his friend raped her.

I nodded again, leaned forward, and clasped my hands on the desk. "I'm sure there are capable attorneys in Atlanta or even Nashville that would jump at the opportunity to represent Dallas Davenport."

"I don't like how his attorney is handling the case," Kavion said, shaking his head. "It's already tough enough being in the limelight, but the media circus is making a mockery of his image and our team.

"When I saw you last night, I knew Dallas needed someone like you representing him, not a wannabe fame chaser."

"Well thank you, Kavion, for the complement. I'm willing to look into the case. Sounds interesting enough, but

Dallas will have to make that call himself. If he's serious, tell him to call me."

I couldn't allow Kavion to leave without knowing how he's been personally. I remembered hearing on the gossip shows that he and his long-time relationship with actress Camille White ended when she was caught leaving the hotel with her co-star Davis Knox.

While Kavion and I were in college, his mother and I never got along because she thought I was never good enough for her son—typical for most mothers who try making mama's boys out of their sons. She only saw me as some groupie whose convoluted goal was to siphon her son's money he was likely to make playing football professionally. But she was oblivious to the fact that I already had my own money through my mother's trust fund.

Kavion and I also got into a few disagreements about his mother invading our space despite her being three thousand miles away. I felt her presence in every argument we ever had. So when we broke up, there was no love lost about seeing or speaking to his mother again—twenty years would still be too soon.

"So how is the family? I know some pretty young thing snagged her little claws into you," I inquired.

He tried laughing it off. "I haven't been so lucky. Honestly, I haven't met the right one since we broke up."

"I thought you might give that actress a second chance." I watched him closely; he cringed at the mentioning of her.

"She was definitely a mistake. I cursed myself for ever getting involved with her. Her PR and my PR thought it would be good press," he said. "I'm not being rude, but I would prefer not speaking of Camille at this moment."

A part of me was happy to hear that little piece of news. I, too, had not found anyone that stood up to Kavion's level of intimacy. He was the one person I always thought what if things were different.

I stood up and began walking towards my office door. "Kavion, I'm glad you stopped by. I was on my way to lunch."

Then I posed, "Why don't you join me? We have so much catching up to do."

Damn, it felt good being so assertive. Credit it being in my profession all these years.

"Sure, why not. The tournament is not until tomorrow," he said. "My day is wide open. What place do you have in mind?"

Chapter 32

Cole Kennedy
Charleston, South Carolina

Life can be so complicated.

Old feelings came back strongly, including those that remained unresolved after all these years. I once loved Kavion, but I hated the way we ended our relationship. Yet, I was willing to wipe the slate clear of everything, chalking it up as immaturity.

I did consider whether I'd be making the mistake of letting him back in my life only for him to walk away. Especially if he did not feel that spark or connection; however, I felt no more struggle.

The invitation to visit Kavion at the Charleston Place Hotel was more than tempting. I had to see him. And I knew that I could not deny myself an opportunity to find out whether it might work again.

Riding the elevator to the seventh floor, I was a nervous wreck for probably all the right but lustful reasons. I stood there shifting from one foot to the other until the door opened.

He was in room No. 710, a luxurious presidential suite. He opened the door as soon as I knocked. My knees buckled at the site of him standing in the signature white hotel robe.

His smooth chest peeked through the terry cloth, glistening in the night's light. He greeted me with a warm hug, and he invited me inside.

"I just stepped out the shower," he said.

I swear I did not want to let him go. He smelled so fresh, so fuckable.

"I almost did not show up," I blurted, just as he released his embrace.

Taking a step backward, he looked at me out the corner of his eye. That was something I loved how his eyes always seem to smile at me.

"I'm glad you changed your mind. Have a seat. Better yet, why don't you pour yourself a drink while I finish getting dressed? Make me whatever you're having."

I walked over to the bar while he walked toward the bedroom.

"Where should we go?" he shouted.

I imagined his naked body atop of mine and my legs securing themselves around his muscular torso. I wanted to tell him that we could skip the pretentious acts of two people out on a date and go straight to where we both want to be — in bed, fucking.

Instead, I suggested we go to a nearby Japanese Bar & Grill off Waterfront Park. Deep inside, I wanted to know if Kavion was the same guy I knew more than ten years ago.

People change. Shit, I've changed. I wanted to know if there was still something between us or if I'd wasted my time fantasizing over the sparks I felt earlier today.

In a matter of moments, Kavion returned to the living room area wearing a black pair of slacks and a grey button-down shirt, and carrying a black and grey plaid blazer. Although he was fully dressed, his swagger and sexiness allowed me to see past the materials of clothing that concealed his immaculate body.

My pussy had a mind of its own, and it screamed for his attention. The moistness from my pussy and the throbbing of my clit excited me. Meanwhile, I handed Kavion the drink; it was obvious he rather have a drink of me instead.

"I wanted to do this all day and if I don't act on my instinct now, I will never know." Kavion's voice was raspy and deep. He grabbed me close to his chest. We stood staring not knowing if the other should lead with that initial kiss. Our eyes told a story of two lovers longing to be with each other.

I was past gone. My pussy ached for that special attention, and I didn't blame her. She had not been acquainted with a real, virile dick in several months. The double-shot of tequila made my body flush looking into his large dark eyes with long dark eyelashes that any woman would kill to have naturally.

Kavion bent down and kissed me softly on the lips. My eyes fluttered then closed. This time, I stepped in closer, pressing my pussy against his harden glory. I draped my arms around his neck, and he went down for seconds.

That kiss took me back to the year 2001—the year we confessed our love. The arguing and the making up and the time apart were erased away. It seemed only months instead of more than ten years. That kiss reminded why I could never find another man to replace Kavion.

Those lips, so full, covered mine with passion. He licked and sucked mine as if I was his favorite flavor. Now, both sets of lips were swollen. I was surprised that I managed to pull away. I had freshened up as much as I could, but honestly, I needed a cold shower before leaving his suite.

The concierge service arranged a car to pick us up at the front entrance of the hotel. As we waited for the car, a few people in the lobby recognized him. He handled his fans with love and respect. I always remembered him being never too famous or too busy to talk to his fans or give autographs. It never surprised me that he'd been loved for so long.

After a couple of hours at the restaurant, we walked around Waterfront Park. Kavion then suggested we go back to his place for coffee. I agreed to join him, but I told him that I couldn't stay long.

"I have to be at the pier by 2:30. I've been putting off this cruise for some time now."

"You lost the bet. You said that whatever I want, goes. And I want you to spend the night with me."

"Don't be so subtle," I mocked.

"If I wasn't dedicated to the golf tournament, I would leave with you in a heartbeat," he said. "Cole, I've missed you. I've always thought about you. I was too afraid to contact you in fear you would reject me, or that you were married with children. Especially after the way our relationship ended so long ago.

"But spending the day with you confirms that what we had is still there. I'm willing to give it a chance—I mean, if you're not dating anyone serious. But I really think we should try to get to know each other again."

Kavion did not hide the desperate tone in his voice. He went into the full kitchen and returned with a bottle of Evian water and two glasses. We then sat down together on the plush sofa.

"You've been thinking about it this long?" I asked, while he poured into both glasses; he then handed me a glass.

"More than you would ever know." He looked into my eyes as if they were searching for the same realization. I would not admit it. At least not yet, anyway. "Would you like some espresso?"

I tried turning away from his magnetism, my heart beating through my sheer blouse. I had never wanted a man more than I wanted Kavion at that moment. I did not care if his words were empty promises or just games to get me in his bed.

Why am I acting as if I did not want this? I've been fantasizing about him ever since we broke up. He was my first real relationship. He was my first real love. Everyone before and after him were just shameful imitations.

"I would like a double-shot," I finally answered.

I took off my jacket and hung it on the back of the bar stool. It was getting quite warm, so I unbuttoned the top button, trying to cool the heat that emanated from my body. I was glad I stuffed two condoms in my purse earlier. I hopped on the stool and watched him operate the gourmet machine. I smiled at how comfortable he was in the kitchen.

"Can I help you with anything?" I asked.

"No, I've got this."

My mind wondered about all of the possibilities how the night might end in his bed. Meanwhile, I casually walked towards the living room and turned on his iPod. I glanced at the portfolio that lay open on the entertainment unit.

Shortly thereafter, Kavion brought two cups of espresso and I joined him out back in the private garden patio. We engaged in more small talk while we enjoyed the celestial view.

'So what are we doing, Cole?" Kavion blurted out.

"What do you mean?"

I knew exactly what he was implying. There was nothing that stopped me from taking it to the next level. I had no love interest other than my work. Nor was there anything that kept me from jumping over the table and giving him the best pussy of his life.

"Us," he answered, confidently. "Cole, if I could turn back time I would. But I never stopped loving you."

He got up from his seat and pulled me up. We began dancing to imaginary music.

"Kavion, let's just take this one day at a time, but I'm willing to give it a try."

He bent over and kissed me gently. Slowly. He was being himself and the same person that I remembered.

"Are you ready to fuck my brains out?" he whispered; he was always into role playing and I was eager to play his whore.

In one day, my perfectly normal and celibate life was turning into a dream filled with sex, sex, and more sex. I didn't want to seem too ready at the possibility.

So, I grabbed his hand and lead him back inside until we reached the large bedroom with a king size bed. I gently pushed him on the bed.

Undressing him with my eyes, I unhooked the bun and shook my head slowly, allowing my hair to flow against my back. I slowly untied my wrap shirt. I slowly stepped out, revealing my emerald green bra and thong. I straddled him, still wearing my stilettos.

"You want some of this, daddy?" I moaned, while rubbing my pussy lightly.

I unhooked my bra, allowing my appreciable assets to freely move as they pleased; they bounced with each movement I made. I watched Kavion lower his sexy glare upon my titties. He bit down on his bottom lip then caressed my left breast. His lips made a slippery trail around my areolas before they stopped at my hardened nipples.

"Mmm, shit. You miss them, don't you?"

He nodded.

The room became filled with his loud sucking and tasting of my body. I clasped my arms around his neck, nestling my titties into his face. Each flick of his tongue against my flesh had me feeling lighter in the head.

Suddenly, he stopped and glanced up at me seductively. He reached down with his left hand and fumbled at unbuckling his belt. Inwardly, I smiled because I knew he would not be having sex with any groupie. Nor was he Kavion Cottrell the Pro Bowl football star, either.

He stepped out his pants revealing a nice-size package that needed proper handling. It beckoned me to climb on and give him the ride of his life, but I had other plans.

"May I taste it first?" I asked in a slutty tone.

Instinctively, our bodies entwined in one of my favorite positions with him: My head between his thighs and his between mine; we both delved into each other's pleasure spots.

I wasted no time exploring his tool again. It was exactly as I remembered only a little heavier. While he enthusiastically attended to my pussy, I savored his length, smoothness, and thickness. Gently, I stroked his dick up and down; I closed my eyes and moaned. I slowly licked his member as if it were my favorite Häagen-Dazs ice cream on a stick.

"Mmm, you taste so good—"

Our body chemistry was sweet smelling; it was my aphrodisiac. I proceeded to roll a condom on his well-endowed member, which looked as if it was about to explode within the latex material.

I opened my legs, inviting him to partake. He was gentle as he slid inside my soaking wet slit inch by inch by inch. Killing me softly with the song of his stroke.

His moans were caught in his throat, trying to maintain his control. He spoke little. He only concentrated on the act. He was focused on pleasing me as he worked his hips in a circular motion, ensuring that all of me would be satisfied.

I wasn't ready to cum just yet. It felt too good for it to end. I maintained my muscle-gripping stronghold on him. But then his pace slowed; we changed positions. I rolled atop of him while maintaining my hold on him.

With each stroke, I felt him at the base of my stomach, so I slowed it down a bit. The slow dance excited me much sooner than I wanted to surrender. It was hard and the waves of ecstasy rushed through my being.

Chapter 33

Stefan Lewis
Charleston, South Carolina

The sales representative was more than accommodating to me.

"Is there anything else you need?" she inquired.

"Uh, yeah. I would like the card to say, 'I am thinking of you . . . You are on my mind . . . you are in my heart.' I would also like the roses delivered before noon, if that's possible."

"Yes, that is possible."

"Thank you."

I hung up the phone feeling great about myself. I felt brand new. I arrived in Charleston two days ago and already found a place to stay, renting a room among college students. I would definitely need a car if I was to find work. Maybe I'd convince mother to loan me a few more dollars for a used car. There was no way I could get around without my own transportation.

I had a lot to do on my agenda, and I had to familiarize myself in Cole's world if I was to survive as her husband.

She's become some type of celebrity in her community.

I wanted to feel some type of closeness to her, so the first day I landed here I took the thirty-minute stroll to her place of employment. It was a nice, stylish building off the Charleston harbor waters. The waiting area screamed modern with old-money charm. This was the reception area that Cole crossed every day—I closed my eyes imagining the scent of her perfume as she'd float pass me.

I imagined her lightly bumping me while she raced towards the elevator only to drop her briefcase. Papers all over the place, I would bend down and retrieve all of the loose papers. Our hands would brush and then there would be the look of rejoicing once she recognizes me.

She would take the rest of the day off. Shit, maybe the entire week so that we could reconnect the way that lovers do. I wondered if today would be my lucky day.

"Hello, mister. Can I help you with something?" I opened my eyes to the glaring of a twenty-something, somewhat attractive receptionist. Her dark brown hair cascaded over her shoulders with a single streak of bright pink in her bang. Her hair style consisted of loose, flirty curls. Her vibrant green eyes were hidden behind black designer style frames. Maybe out of desperation and in another life I might have given her consideration.

She looked at me with disdain. Apparently, I interrupted her self-manicure.

The once-over made me self-conscious, causing me to look down at myself: I had on khaki shorts, a light pink and green polo shirt, with tan boat shoes. Not something I would wear if I worked at such a place.

I guess I didn't fit the profile of a big-time lawyer or an important client with ample resources at my disposal. Her look said I was nothing more than a regular schmuck, so flirting with her was out of the question.

"Uh, no. I think I'm in the wrong place I'm looking for."

My voice trailed off; I pulled out a piece of paper pretending to look a little lost and I even scratched my head to play on the confusion.

Then I pull out the charm and gave her a toothy smile. She was obviously pleased by my handsome features. I was reminded of my mother, who always said I had the eyes of a charmer.

"Maybe I can help you." Her voice softened. "I'm Phoebe." She extended her small, manicured hand, which was smooth to the touch. I also noticed a large oval diamond pave ring on her right index finger.

"Yes, I'm looking for 1108 Harvard View Drive—"

"Oh, I see how you can make that mistake; this is 1108 Harbor View Drive." She tore a piece of paper and drew a small map for me. "It's actually three streets over."

"Thanks for your help."

I was about to walk out dutifully, but then I had a change of mind.

"Uh, Phoebe," I said, turning around. "I hope I'm not being too forward. But I was hoping you would want to hang out with me tonight. This is my first night in town and I would really enjoy your company."

Oh, well. I lied.

Without any second thought, she pulled out a business card from the display and wrote her cell phone number on the back of it. "Sure, I would love to. I get off at 5:30 p.m., so any time after eight would be great with me."

The way she ogled at me, I knew she would be easy to unwrap all the information I needed on Cole. What better way than the receptionist at the law firm.

I returned to my hangout and mulled about how I would ease into her life. I could spend all day dreaming about her, our life together, and how happy we would finally be.

Cole's lifestyle would take some getting used to. The parties, charity events, traveling across the world, bumping shoulders with decision makers could be overwhelming. But I would sacrifice my career and my life if it meant spending the rest of my life as her husband and her lover—I would go to hell and back ten times, no, a hundred, for Cole.

The gala was two days away, and I had a lot to do for our big reunion. I needed to rent a limousine and reserve a room at the hotel just in case we could not wait to indulge with each other's body.

Also, I found a tuxedo shop off King Street for the party on Friday. Cole's going to be so surprised when I pick her up; she'd probably die of excitement.

Her soft arms wrapped around my neck, adorning me with sweet kisses, I could feel her getting warm between her legs. Then she'd be begging me to extinguish the fire that had been raging in her for ten years. And I'd accommodate her desire by making tender love to her.

Not the stuff inspired by porn. Just sweet, passionate love to my soul mate—my woman.

The evening with Phoebe turned out to be a waste of my time. She showed me The Market and we went by The Aquarium. Then we stopped by a music store and played chess at one of the tables.

When pressed, she could not give me any more information on Cole than what had been written in a local newspaper article. She did not even have Cole's home address or cell phone number.

"I'm just curious. Why are you asking me all these questions about Ms. Kennedy?"

I was prepared for something like that.

"To be honest, I'm considering to ask her to represent me in my case against the state."

Fortunately, she did not make any more of a deal out of it. We bade each other goodbye several minutes later. Humph, good riddance.

By Friday, I was worried that I would not be able to accompany her to the gala. I made plans to pick her up in the limo, but I could never reach her at her office. Her assistant—

he sounded like some intellectual punk ass—told me a couple of times that she was out of town.

"I-I . . . I really need to get in contact with her," I pleaded.

"Okay, if you really need to get in contact with her, may I ask what the nature of your business is?"

"Look, I already told you," I said, sighing. "I have a lawsuit that I would like for Ms. Kennedy to represent on my behalf. But I would prefer speaking with her about it."

"I'm sorry. Ms. Kennedy is out of town," he answered. "But I will need some specifics."

"Oh, forget it."

Then I hung up. I resolved to myself once Cole and I were married, I would see to it that his ass was fired.

Chapter 34

Cole Kennedy
Charleston, South Carolina

My trip to the Bahamas was liberating. I should have taken a vacation years ago. It was a cure to stress that I would recommend to all of my friends.

The look in my eyes had said it all when I stepped off the ship at the Port of Nassau. There he was, dressed in an off-white linen pantsuit, holding a bouquet of white roses.

Kavion surprised me by meeting me at Nassau port. His plan was to "kidnap" me to Paradise Island. He had reserved a suite at the Atlantis Hotel. What was supposed to have been merely the last two days of my cruise, I spent them with Kavion reconnecting with one another.

Between fucking each other's brains out and rediscovering our bodies, we reconnected with each other on a spiritual and an intimately personal level. We decided to take our relationship slow but also be monogamous. Being that it would be a long-distance relationship, we promised we would see each other at least twice a month.

I returned to Charleston floating. I felt as if I'd become the luckiest woman in the world. That's right, Cole Kennedy had gotten her groove back, and it felt so damn good. I had once thought I would have spent the best years of my life as a single, lonely woman.

This was something too good to keep to myself.

"Are you sure you want me to go?" Kavion asked.

"I asked you, didn't I?" I retorted; I still could not contain my giddiness. "Of course I want you to come along."

He pulled me into his arms, walking prouder than any conqueror on a football field. "Yeah, I'm just making sure no one has eyes for my woman."

"Even if someone did, my eyes can't keep you out of my mind." I kissed him while we waited for my plane to board from Atlanta's Hartsfield-Jackson International Airport.

"My flight lands in Charleston at 4:35 p.m. I can have a car service take me to your place," he said. "I know you have a lot to prepare for tonight."

He kissed me again—I swear I did not want to let go. I was enjoying this fantasy: My prince had swept me off my feet; nothing like this happened in real life.

"Maybe you can show me a few new tricks before this shindig."

He winked at me before he kissed me goodbye. I hesitated releasing my hold on him. I stood there and touched my lips long after he disappeared into the throng of people hustling and bustling to catch their flights.

* * *

Being away from work for seven solid days meant that I had to go by the office this weekend just to respond to the countless e-mails and correspondences.

On second thought, I figured that maybe I could pick up the snail mail at the law firm and later open the e-mails from home. Besides, I had a sneaking suspicion that I would not be in the mood to travel after another intense night with Kavion.

I arrived at my office ten minutes after ten. There were flowers on my desk probably to congratulate me for the honors. I shuffled through the stacks of mail, petitions, and motions. Jabree had already weaned out the most important mail from the mail that could wait a few days. I checked a few voice messages, which were mostly congratulatory. I figured that I would see most of my colleagues later, so I would not have to return their calls.

Monty called that he had some developing news in his godson's case. There were also a few hang-ups. And the last one was a caller who whispered my name, but the tone freaked me out so much that I deleted it without thinking. I gathered my belongings and headed home—and I hoped to get some rest before Kavion arrived.

* * *

Kavion arrived at my condominium a few minutes after six. We had two-and-a-half hours to get ready before the yacht left the dock.

My hair was pinned up with curls and my French manicured hands and feet were perfect. All I needed to do was apply my makeup and slip on my designer dress. I offered to place his belongings in my guest room.

"You know what, I'm looking forward to sleep in my big ol' bed all weekend long," he said.

I joked, "I wouldn't count on that so fast."

We both kissed before I allowed him to get situated while I finished dinner: something simple, as in grilled salmon with a raspberry glaze; rice pilaf, and steamed asparagus.

When he emerged from my bedroom wearing black silk lounge pants and matching black tank top, I almost said "fuck the party; we can celebrate by ourselves." Instead, I handed him a glass of Pinot Grigio.

"I can get use to this," he said, beaming, as he accepted the glass.

"Well, I believe in keeping my man happy."

I started to walk away, but Kavion pulled me back into his arms.

"Is that what I am to you?"

He pulled me closer and tantalized me with an erotic kiss. I parted my lips and darted my tongue inside of his. I was losing myself inside that kiss. There was nothing I'd rather do than to jump his bone, but my hair was at stake. It would have been rude to skip out on a party where I was an honoree, but I was that close.

Coming up for air, I said, "Isn't that what you want, to be my man? You told me yourself you wanted us to try to make it work."

Now, that was something I needed to get used to: Having a man in my home; the first and only man I had ever loved. My feelings for him were moving too fast. I reminded myself that it had been more than a decade since we last parted ways, a break up that tore me to the core. A relationship that left me in a never-ending pursuit of happiness for myself. Happiness I never found. Until now. I laughed at the irony.

Then I began entertaining a poignant reality: When would I have time for a relationship?

Maybe the distance would be something good. I could not afford to change my routine because Kavion walked back into my life.

That sounded weird. However, when I looked over a Kavion sipping the last of the wine, and how temptingly and delicious he looked, I reasoned that I could definitely get use to him being in my life, and in my bed.

Compared to the other boats, the yacht on which the awards ceremony was hosted was like a snapshot from one of those lifestyles of the rich and famous shows. It was one hundred and twenty-five feet long, sleek, and named Black Beauty. It was owned by a local businessman who was a past client of our firm.

When I walked through the doors, it was as if the world had become a slow-motion movie premier, and Kavion and I were stars walking the red carpet as everyone stopped, stared, or gawked at the beautiful couple. I wore a royal blue Tori Cabaret one-shoulder sequence cocktail dress while Kavion wore an all-black pin-striped Armani suite and matching black shoes.

The event turned out to be a who's who in Charleston. Everyone from the mayor to a couple of state representatives were in attendance.

I would have loved if some of the people in attendance had taken a moment to notice how beautiful I looked or how exquisite my dress complemented the curves of my body. But I did not mind being in the background watching Kavion interact with so many people.

He was so genuine, attentive, and being fine as hell as he was made me hornier than a fraternity member at a cathouse. We eventually spent the night at the Charleston Place Hotel, which was where we first reconnected.

Chapter 35

Stefan Lewis
Charleston, South Carolina

I felt like a fucking fool.

I moved across the country to be with Cole, and she's already parading around town with another man. She refused to answer my calls because she'd already made plans.

Why would she jeopardize what we had going for some cheap fling?

I tried making sense of what happened. Maybe it's true that she does not know I'm here, but that does not give her an excuse to run around town with someone who's probably filled her head with a bunch of sweet nothings.

What would her colleagues think of her? A woman of her stature should not be seen with men that are not her husband. This would be embarrassing if this gets back to mother.

That bitch!

I couldn't understand why she needed an escort, and I couldn't help wondering if there was more going on. She and her "escort" walked so close I thought they were conjoined twins attached at the hip. He whispered something in her ear and she giggled and playfully swatted the air just as they walked on the enormous boat.

That fucking bitch!

Maybe she really didn't know that I was in town, and she needed someone to accompany her to that party. Maybe that's not her fault. But in the back of my mind, this scenario reminded me so much of Fiona and her indiscretions. That bullying muscle head . . . No, I better not revisit how she betrayed me. It does nothing for my blood pressure, which I felt spiking once I saw that man with Cole.

Surely, Cole would not be anything like that other bitch who rightfully should remain as a long, long afterthought in my life.

I called myself being gentlemanly by not wanting to make a scene. However, I felt as if I had inexplicably lost a million dollars while I watched that boat leave the dock. Feeling helpless, I debated whether I should stay, knowing there was the possibility someone might think I was a prowler.

Doesn't Cole know, being my fiancée, it's been my responsibility to be concerned about our fidelity to each other? That trust is one of the pillars of a relationship?

God, I can't believe I'm calling her a bitch!

I glanced at my watch. It was only ten o'clock. Shit, I could not go home yet, because I had already told my roommates that I was supposed to be with Cole and I would not return until late. I didn't need their pity or laughter.

I noticed there were a few bars nearby that I could hang out until the boat returned to the dock. I suppose it would only be a couple of hours. Then I could double back and make sure she does not go home with her escort or do anything she might regret.

I thought I would go out of my mind wondering what Cole was up to on that boat. However, I was entertained by a few of the female patrons that were bold and had no shame in their game approaching me.

A larger-framed woman with a reasonably pretty face copped a seat next to me while I sat at the bar. "I would love to see what's in those jeans," she cooed into my ear.

For a moment, I almost asked for my check and considered leaving with her. It had been since before my time in that facility since I last been with a woman. And I'd been so focused on reuniting with my fiancée that I even ceased to consider taking matters into my own hands.

"Really?" I responded, dryly.

"Humph, I see that you must be preoccupied or something. Have a nice life."

You too, I muttered to myself.

After I'd returned from the bathroom, another woman approached me and commented on my eyes.

"Has anyone ever told you that you look like an actor?' she inquired.

I took a sip from my club soda; I knew that I had to remain mentally sharp for Cole's sake. "Thank you for the compliment, but I'm just here to kill some time. I'm supposed to be meeting up with my fiancée for a late-night date."

She curled her upper lip at me and walked off. "You sound a little gay to me—"

Yeah, whatever!

I found it amusing that I literally had to fight off these desperate women with a stick. Cole should feel fortunate that I've been a faithful man—I hope for her sake that she's remained the same.

It was 11:15 p.m. when I returned to the harbor. I tried to stay as inconspicuous as possible. I did not want to be perceived as a troubled lonely man sitting at a pier waiting for his woman who left him behind while she attended a party.

My mind was in a million places. How could a relationship grow without trust? Right now, I didn't trust her.

When I thought about how Cole interacted with her date, I thought I sensed something unsettling: She was in high spirits and obviously enjoying her company.

I did not see a woman upset—or at the very least, preoccupied—about not being with her fiancé. I simply did not want her in a state where she might be wrongly influenced. That could end badly for her.

The boat returned to the harbor just as midnight approached. It was a picture and work of beauty. It glided upon the water like a whisper; I barely heard it part the water.

I almost did not see them when they exited the ramp. She was wearing his jacket over her shoulders. They walked hugging while they went down the ramp. I tried to blend among the late-night crowd as best as I could, and I made sure that I stayed a few steps behind.

They hopped into a black Town Car. There were a few cabs waiting to pick up potential riders, so I got in the first cab that appeared ready to go. The aroma of fried chicken wafted, a reminder that I had not eaten since lunch. My stomach growled so loud the driver glanced at me via his rearview mirror.

"Where to, boss?" asked the cab driver, who was middle aged and fair skinned; he wore his long black hair pulled back into a greasy ponytail. He also wore a too-tight yellow and white Hawaiian style shirt whose seam was held together by the strands. From where I sat, he never worked out a day in his life. His body was a lumpy mass of molten flesh. It was as if he was lying down in the driver's seat.

I handed him a hundred-dollar bill. "And I'll pay the cost of the ride. I just need you to follow that car. My fiancée is in that car—"

The driver chortled. "It's been a long time since someone asked me to follow a car." He revved up the engine. "As long as you don't involve me in some bullshit, I can do that." He made eye contact with me through his rearview mirror.

I was quick to reason to myself just what kind of help this fucking glob of a health risk could possibly be to me? He couldn't get out the car fast enough for me to even consider asking for his help.

"I just need you for this," I told him.

He punched the accelerator and made up a reasonable amount of distance. He offered, "I'm Big Mike" before he stuffed the crisp bill in his shirt pocket.

"Lewis," I countered.

"So how long she's been creeping around?" He attempted to make eye contact with me again through his rearview mirror. His eyes were beady and he appeared creepy, but I sensed he was harmless.

Humph, a harmless fat fuck at that.

"Hopefully, she's not. She thinks I'm out of town, and I just need to know I can trust her."

"I see." He reached over to his right and began toying around with his iPad. He placed an earphone plug in his right ear and began bobbing his head. It was so loud that I actually recognized it being The Starship's "We Built This City." He got so carried away that I thought he'd become Mickey Thomas, who was the group's lead singer at the time.

Big Mike turned out to be a beast on the road. What he lacked in physical fitness, he compensated for it behind the wheel. He artfully bobbed in and out of traffic until we were directly behind the luxury car. We followed them for another mile down Meeting Street until we were in the turning lane into Charleston Place Hotel. He turned down the radio.

"Um, boss, the car is turning into the hotel's valet parking. Do you want me to follow in pursuit?" He was enjoying the game of cat-and-mouse whereas I, on the other hand, fumed.

"No, just park over there, thank you." I then pointed to the nearby parking meter. "Give me ten minutes and keep the meter running. I'll be right back."

I had to know. I had to see with my own two eyes if she was really cheating on me.

Nevertheless, I had to make sure that she was not spending the night in this hotel. I walked into the lobby just as they entered the elevator. She had just turned and entered into his embrace for a hug.

That fucking bitch!

It was clearly evident that she was more than eager to give him what was mine, and what I had gone through as a victim of the goddamned legal system by defending her honor. They appeared so disgustingly cozy and comfortable. He was tall with an athletic build—there was something about him that was so familiar.

I snapped my finger.

Oh shit! I mouthed silently.

How could I ever forget that was Cole's ex-boyfriend from college? My heart dropped to the fucking floor; it had been stomped on.

I walked over to the receptionist. She was finishing her last transaction.

"Hello, do you have reservations?" She was polite and smiled at me.

"Ummm, was that?" I asked, pointing towards the elevator door.

"Kavion Cottrell. Yes, he and his wife are here for the weekend," she said.

His wife? This could not be happening. I'm going to kill that bitch and that motherfucker!

"Sir, do you have reservations?" she inquired again; her smile had disappeared because there was a line that had formed behind me.

"Ummm, I'm sorry. I just changed my mind about staying here."

She looked at me as if I just got off the short bus. I excused myself and rushed out of the lobby bumping into a couple of people along the way. The last person I bump had even cursed at me.

"Watch where the fuck you're going —"

"Sorry," I responded without looking back.

Once I reached the parking lot, I spotted the nearest light post and walked over there. I tried catching my breath because I felt as if I was hyperventilating. It seemed everything around me began spinning.

No . . . no . . . no . . . no . . . Not again!

I struggled badly to keep my emotions intact. I realized that I had been made a fool of again.

Come on, calm down . . .

I tried repeating to myself that I could handle this setback. I could handle Cole; however, I was enraged. Once again, I was a victim of tricks and circumstances. Cole will wish that she never fucked around on me.

I damned near gave up my life for her. Actually, I gave up everything for her. I was locked away for ten years because of her. I helped her by ridding her attackers, and all I've gotten in return is a kick in the balls.

That bitch. That fucking bitch!

"Well, I am not going to sit here and let some motherfucker claim my woman," I proclaimed aloud to myself.

I checked my composure and walked back to the taxi. I plopped myself in the back seat and gave Big Mike the address to my apartment.

"I take it she's been a bad girl." Big Mike said. "I suspect that since you've not volunteered any information—"

"Yeah, I guess you can say that," I replied, sighing; I then put my focus out the window so he could not make eye contact with me through his rearview mirror.

Yes, I was crushed and hurt beyond repair. There was only vengeance in my heart.

"Well it's her loss. You are a nice looking young man. I am sure all the ladies will be happy to hear you're on the market again. I'll tell you what, men are always getting the bad rap and they say seventy-five percent of us cheat?

"Humph. The woman cheated in every relationship I know of. They're always thinking the grass is greener on the other side . . . Uh-huh, that's why I'll stay single until the day I die."

Big Mike then picked up a chicken leg and practically shoved the entire drumstick in his mouth.

Actually, you're single 'cause you're a fat, greasy slob. I bet you've forgotten what your dick looked like because you can't see it.

I sat in silence the remainder of my ride. I paid Big Mike the fare and returned to my room.

I was glad my roommates had retired for the night so I did not have to put on a front. I headed for my room and stripped out of my clothing. I washed my face, brushed my teeth, and plopped on the bed. I was lying there thinking about all the possible ways I could get back at Cole. Like how I was going to make her pay for making me look like a fool. I honestly thought things were different with Cole. I always felt like she was the one for me. Yet she turned out to be just like the rest.

* * *

I wouldn't say I have a split personality; it's more of an alter ego. That's where I get my strength when there is complete chaos in my life.

It's like something inside me takes over. When I'm hurt and I'm tired of feeling the pain, I allow my alter ego to have his way. All I have to do is sit back from the sidelines and watch my worries disappear.

This is the part of the game I enjoy the most. Especially knowing that I would be the last person ever to see Cole. It was her betrayal that caused this hatred for her.

Whenever the thrill of controlling someone else's destiny is presented, something within me takes over.

Sometimes, love has made me do things that I've hated. I'm a passionate man, and I've only done things out of love. However, the problem with loving someone so much is that it's made me do crazy things.

It's been suggested that I've needed anger management. Once, my mother warned me that it could send me behind bars.

Too late. Been there, done that.

When there's no hope, love can create the type of monsters mothers warn their sons about becoming. The type of monster that cannot let go or handle the pain of rejection. The type of monster that believes in his world so much that he would do everything in his power to make it his reality, regardless if he wanted it or not.

To win at life, adversity has to be encountered, fought, and ultimately defeated. There is no other way. No options. One either beats it, or be beaten.

Sounds simple, right?

Chapter 36

Cole Kennedy
Atlanta, Georgia

I needed to go over the strategy with Kavion's friend Dallas Davenport. Having my latest case in Georgia was perfect because I could handle two matters at once. By that, I'd conduct business defending my client by day and satisfy my kitty at night in the arms of the man that I loved.

Since accepting this case, I've had to deal with the paparazzi. The media had already been speculating my relationship with Kavion, but now elements of sensationalism involving a high-profiled professional athlete fed their curiosity.

The petitioner in the paternity lawsuit was Karan Mitchell. She was a housekeeper at the Renaissance Hotel in Memphis, Tennessee. In her complaint, she stated that she first met Dallas at a girlfriend's house in Atlanta who was dating professional basketball player Mitch Wallace at the time.

Karan claimed that she and Dallas hit it off that night, and they began seeing each other casually ever since. Months later, she found out she was pregnant. She claimed he wanted her to have an abortion once she told him she was pregnant. Their relationship fizzled because an abortion was against her religious beliefs.

Yet, having sex out of wedlock was okay?

What piqued my interest in the case was the fact that she also claimed that Dallas raped her, and that was how her twins were conceived. Instead of filing criminal charges, she sued him for $10 million plus $20,000 a month for child support.

She then stated that her twin sons were now ten months old and Dallas had done nothing for their children. And although the children were conceived through a violent act, she claimed she still loved him because he's the children's father.

"I forgave him because he was drunk," she said. "But I should not be faced with raising my two sons alone struggling and broke while their father is a millionaire football player living the high life.

"I did not ask for the card that I've been dealt, but I'm going to make it right by my children."

What sent her over the edge, she said, was when he claimed they never had any type of physical relationship.

I found it ironic that I would agree to defend somebody accused of rape. I've not remembered much of what happened to me, but only bits and pieces. Flashes of Barry Kinloch atop of me while his friends held me down were about as much as I've recalled after all these years. At best, I remembered not being able to breathe and hyperventilating once I was fully cogent of my situation.

That's remained a touchy topic, but I've never allowed it to define me and what I've become in life.

Since I arrived in Charleston, I've volunteered my time at the rape crisis center twice a month, and I've offered legal services to victims of crime. I also started the St. Marie Foundation in memory of Deidra St. Marie, a sixteen-year-old honor student who was drugged with rufilin and raped by classmates. Later, she was unmercifully tormented by girls, who bullied her following the vicious attack.

She could not take the abuse and committed suicide a month later. I learned to deal with being a survivor of rape, but most like Deidra do not—it took me years of counseling before I could forgive Barry and the others for their crimes.

* * *

I had a knack for spotting bullshit, and Karan Mitchell's pores were overflowing with it. I first saw through her lies during her deposition.

In situations like this, the more they talk the more likely they would trip up. Her constant craving for attention had put a foot straight in her mouth, but I needed confirmation and I hoped that's where her friend Natalie Dunn would come in.

In her complaint, Karan said she never met Dallas before that night. But she contradicted herself when she claimed they secretly saw each other for a couple of months. What I don't like is women crying rape for attention or revenge. These false accusations take away from the real victims—like Deidra.

I needed someone competent with this case. I had worked with legal assistant Sasha Terrell a few times over the years, and she did an awesome job. I asked one of the managing partners from the firm, Autry Brown, to lend Sasha's talent until the trial's completion.

"I need you to accompany me to the deposition of Natalie Dunn," I told her. "I'm almost positive that I'll find what I'm looking for. There's something odd about the time of conception that's bothered the hell out of me."

"I guess your client is saying that he was not there?"

"That's right. You know how you listen to your client for certain things—"

"Most of the time."

"I, uh, I really don't think he was there."

I liked the way Sasha and I clicked instantly. She was excited about the trial. We agreed to meet at my office once I returned to Charleston.

The following Tuesday, she came into my office carrying what seemed like weeks' worth of mail rather than what was actually just one day.

"I hope you don't mind since I was coming to your office, I picked up your mail from the mail room," she said, handing me the large stack.

I shuffled through it and it was the usual—orders, requests, thank you cards, junk mail, but one in particular caught my eyes. It was a large manila envelope. It was ordinary yet very mysterious. There was no return address, but the postage originated from Southern California.

I wondered whether this was from the same person who sent a letter to Sydney. I knew it would have to wait until Sasha left before I opened it.

A phone call to Monty seemed more than realistic. If Sydney's assumption was right, I'd be next on the list to be blackmailed and I'll be damned if I'd allow a motherfucker take a dime of my hard-earned money.

I recalled the last phone conversation I had with Sydney two weeks ago. She blurted out that she received a letter in the mail earlier that day. In the letter, the moron demanded fifty-thousand dollars, or else he was going to the cops.

"I told you they would never stop," I reacted. "Today, it's fifty thousand. Next week it will be a hundred. I told you it would never quit with these people."

"I don't know, but I don't want to find out, either." She paused before continuing. "I don't know where I could come up with that type of money.

"Cole, we need to come up with fifty-thousand dollars or else they will contact the police."

"Say what?" I was truly agitated by her inference. "Sydney, you were the last person with The Cyclone before he OD'd on cocaine."

I laughed at the amount. "Some people honestly believe fifty-thousand dollars is get-rich money. Unless they were planning to invest it in an amazing stock, they would be broke by the end of the year."

I noticed that Sasha had returned in my office, breaking my train of thought.

"Cole, is everything all right?"

Sighing, I told her that I had a lot on my mind, but I did not divulge that it was now split between a potential black mailer and the upcoming trial.

"I have something good to share with you. The date Karan Mitchell claimed was conception does not add up with Dallas and Kavion's deposition. Is it possible that he slept with her before he left for the Pro Bowl in Hawaii?"

She explained this was a key in the case and if we could find that missing piece, there was a chance for victory.

"After reviewing the deposition of Dallas and then of Karan, someone is definitely lying," Sasha concluded.

"When is the deposition scheduled for Karan's friend Natalie Dunn?" I inquired. "Maybe she can shed some light on all this after all; Karan does claim that Natalie introduced them."

Sasha said Natalie's deposition was scheduled for the following Thursday afternoon. Usually, these things were scheduled for two days, but we might get everything we needed on Thursday.

"I already booked our flights to Atlanta for Wednesday night so that we could have plenty of time to prepare." She also handed me the itinerary. "We will be busy as a bee."

Chapter 37

Sasha Terrell
Charleston, South Carolina

I was excited about working with Cole Kennedy. I admired her hustle by making partner before the age of forty. I also respected her game and tenacity.

I had been around lawyers who were condescending to paralegals and secretaries. That was never the case with Cole. She made everyone feel like her equal. She always asked for my opinion, and I never heard her talk down to anyone. Not anyone. Not even when a cleaning lady broke her crystal awards plaque while she clumsily dusted in her office.

So when my boss Autry Brown said that Cole had asked me to help work her case, I jumped at the opportunity. I was thrilled, no, honored and I wanted to put my all into this case.

I felt more than at ease around her while we discussed preparing for the case—I still could not believe just how receptive she really was.

"Ms. Kennedy, unless we can get something concrete to back up our client's story, I just don't see us winning the case. Has Monty been able to find any information on Ms. Mitchell that we can't find through a legal search?"

I was thrown off by her shaking her head, causing me to stop in mid-sentence.

"It's Cole, but go ahead—"

"Sure, Ms., uh, I mean Cole." Now I had to pause and gather my thoughts.

"Maybe a deep Web search. There, we are privy to all her social networks, et cetera. Anything to discredit her character would be our best chance."

"Yes, Sasha, we're obvious on the same page." She chortled "Actually, Monty called earlier today and he's stilling working on a lead. Let's meet Sunday afternoon at my house to go over some game plans. I'll fix my famous Thai stir-fry."

"That's fine with me," I responded.

I left work feeling on top of the world. I have been waiting for an opportunity to prove my worth at the firm, and I just may get that chance working with Cole.

Life's great.

My fiancé Savon's business was rapidly expanding. Recently, he landed service contracts with Enterprise and Hertz rental cars, which was nothing short of a huge accomplishment.

Not only will I have the wedding of my dreams, we'll also afford the honeymoon to Hawaii. I'm so giddy. Eight days of sun, surf, and sex. It can't get any better.

Chapter 38

Cole Kennedy
Charleston, South Carolina

After Sasha left my office, I returned my attention back to the mail, particularly the mysterious manila envelope mailed from Southern California.

My hands were shaky as I picked the package up from its corner with two fingers and held it up to the light. I located the envelope opener and ripped through the envelope. There was a single page of paper with letters and words cut from newspapers to convey the message:

Remember Malibu. You thought you got away with murder? $50,000 will keep me quiet. I will contact you with further instructions.

The knock on the door startled me. I dropped the paper on to the floor. It landed near my feet. I kicked it under the desk then I managed a weak "come in."

Whew!

It was Jabree. My heart rate slowed a little. I really don't know what's going on with me. It seems like I'm being paranoid all the time, and I've become suspicious of everything. First, the calls with the heavy breathing, and now this. If someone was trying to spook me they succeeded. But not for long. I needed to get a handle on this situation. I felt like everything was closing in and swallowing me up.

Sydney and her shit reminded me of everything I ran away from. I've come too far for some blackmailer to take it all away. Because if I give in to their initial demand, I might not ever get rid of them.

"You must have impressed someone last night," I heard Jabree say to me; my mind was still in a fog.

He approached my desk with a vase filled with beautiful white lilies with purple carnations. I finally looked up at him.

"Cole, apparently you haven't heard a word I said."

"I'm sorry, what were you saying?"

Jabree laughed hard. His infectious laugh snapped me out of my temporary funk. He now had me smiling both inwardly and outwardly.

"I said you have admirer. This is the second bouquet of flowers you've received from your secret admirer." He took the card from its holder and read the message.

"I am thinking of you . . . You are on my mind . . . You are in my heart—are these from your new beau?"

He winked at me. "I have to admit. I haven't seen you this distracted since . . ." He paused and gazed up at the ceiling, trying to recall. He shook his head, laughing, "Since never."

I stood up and snatched the card from his hand. After studying the message, I noticed it was not signed by anyone.

"I'll thank Kavion when I see him again. I don't have time for this I have work to do." I then shooed him with an out-the-door hand gesture.

"Oh, Jabree—"

He turned around just as he left my office.

"Yes ma'am?"

"You forgot the door." I gave him a playful wink before I returned to burying myself into my work.

* * *

First on my list, I called a colleague who practiced in San Diego. Meredith Cerrito was a lifesaver when she suggested I contact a private investigator she used for her clients, Albert Shaw, formerly a detective on the San Diego police force who now headed a security consultant firm.

It dawned upon me that I had been in South Carolina too long. Being laid back had been a lazy southern drawl filled with a lot of "y'all" and "you know" and "sweet tea" and talk about college football with the state's two major universities. But Mr. Shaw's surfer-like tone reminded me of what I had been exposed to during my college years. Thoughts of eating at In-N-Out Burger ordering a double-double burger without cheese and fries had me feeling nostalgic.

"So tell me, Cole, do you have any idea what the letters are about?" he inquired.

Sighing, I answered, "Before I explain anything about the letters, I gotta tell you about my history with the person who alerted me about these letters of blackmail."

"Sure. Absolutely. Anything that would help."

"First of all, I've known Sydney Starks since I was a student at UCLA. At one point, I almost considered her as a sister I didn't have—"

"Sorry, hate to interrupt. Do you have a phone number or address for her?"

"Yes, I can give that to you before we get off the phone." I found myself recapturing my California dialect as we talked. "As I was saying, Sydney always had a thing for flirting with danger. And she also hung around questionable people. But I liked her. She took an interest in me at a time when I had no friends."

"So you're going to tell me that you was the good girl among the two of you?"

"I guess you can say that. But here's the gist of everything. The blackmailing is over something that happened long ago in Malibu. Sydney may or may not have been the reason why it happened, but I certainly had nothing to do with it. You might say it was being at the wrong place at the wrong time and if anything ever came to light, it might be my words against hers and vice versa."

"I see. Do you know how long these letters have been mailed to you?"

I did not say anything about The Cyclone and his dying of a cocaine overdose; however, I explained to him that Sydney first came to me about receiving e-mails a couple of months ago but she deleted them.

"Is it possible that you might be able to retrieve any information from her e-mail account without her knowledge?" I asked.

"It is possible. Do you have her e-mail address?"

"I'll also give that to you along with the latest phone number and address that I have on her."

"Cool. Hey, do you think she may be involved?"

I took in a deep breath and exhaled slowly. "I don't know what to think. It's just that we were not in contact for over ten years. And then when she calls, it's all about some issue from the past and money. She's already confided in me that she has none and she thinks I'm rolling in it."

"I see. What else do you know about Sydney?" he asked.

"She was recently released from Chowchilla prison serving time for heading a prostitution ring. She said that she did not think to save the first e-mails because they were too creepy. She had to shut down her e-mail and Facebook accounts because of the harassment."

I paused and exhaled again. "That's about it. I can't say that we're that close any more. I just want to get to the bottom of this so I can go on with my life."

"Well, that's what we're going to do. Get to the bottom of this. I'll get back with you in a few days. See you later."

I felt some pressure lifted off my shoulders after I hung up with Mr. Shaw. He also instructed me to mail the note that I just received at once.

I figured that maybe the prints could be lifted off the document, but I hoped that I did not taint it with my clumsiness. I should have been more careful.

Chapter 39

Cole Kennedy
Atlanta, Georgia

Sasha and I arrived in Atlanta on Wednesday, the night before the scheduled deposition of Natalie Dunn. We checked into our hotel rooms and met Dallas and Kavion for dinner in the hotel's restaurant.

I wanted to go over the tactics I had planned to get Ms. Dunn tripped up and contradict Karan Mitchell's story. Dallas thought he should attend the deposition. Although he had the right to be present, I felt his emotional state could affect the outcome, so I convinced him otherwise.

"I've got an investigator tracking Ms. Dunn as we speak," I explained.

"How can someone who never met me lie that I raped her and fathered her children. And I never had sex with that woman?" ranted Dallas, visibly distraught and had been drinking more than the rest of us.

"Dallas, I understand but your reputation is on the line. You've already lost one of your endorsements because of this. I don't think you'd want to lose any more."

Dallas had gestured for a waitress to come by the table. But Kavion intervened.

"Yo', man. I think that's enough. We can't have you being seen drunk in public," he said.

He looked over at Kavion. By then, the waitress had just arrived. He bunched his lips and shook his head.

"I'll just have a water, thank you."

"Sure, I'll be back with a water for you."

I was glad that Kavion had accompanied Dallas. At least there was someone whose opinion Dallas might respect when it came to his drinking.

"So, what about the question of paternity?" he asked.

"You don't need to worry about any paternity test," I said. "We'll prove you're not the father. It's the rape accusations that I'm concerned about at this moment. Even though I believe you, the jury could be swayed by Ms. Mitchell's testimony — your word against hers."

Dallas sat back in his seat and stared down at the table. He shook his head again. "You know, shit like this can drive a person to drinking. For real."

"I understand. But to Ms. Mitchell, you're her meal ticket. That's all this is."

"That's what pisses me off. That's why I'd like to be there so she could tell me in my face that I raped her."

"Again, Dallas. That's not going to help you. You're going to have to trust me on this one."

I noticed that Sasha was preoccupied, she excused herself several times to take personal phone calls. At least she was not acting star struck. She kept it professional, which I liked, but I would have preferred her attention being with our client.

Monty called during dessert. His timing was impeccable as usual.

"Cole, you are sitting down, right?"

"Come on Monty, what do you expect me to be doing?"

"I think I've got what you're looking for in this case involving the football player."

"Great. Meet me in my hotel room in an hour and we'll go over it."

I figured that maybe any piece of good news might calm Dallas down and allow me to do my job as a professional.

After dessert, I cornered Kavion and promised him some midnight loving.

"Baby," I said, looking downward at his prized package, "you know I'll need some male attention after working so hard today. Are you up for it?"

Then I looked up into his eyes. I felt an immediate rise in my body temperature.

"I'm always up for you," he replied, chortling. "Always."

We hugged and kissed, and he gave me a pat on my backside before we walked in opposite directions. Too bad I was in public, or I might have worked it in front of him.

* * *

Monty had a look that was classic. His usual intense demeanor was accentuated by veins that lined his temple was a definite indication that his hard work had paid off. I dared not say it was luck because this was Monty.

He took a seat next to me on the hotel room sofa, and he tossed his note pad on the coffee table in front of us.

"I spotted Karan Mitchell in her beat-up 1995 Honda Civic, and I followed her to a popular eatery where she met up with her girlfriend Natalie Dunn," he said.

He then reached into his vest pocket and showed me his digital voice recorder. He then told me how he managed to secure a booth behind them.

When he turned on the recorder, I was able to identify Karan's voice instantly.

Karan: Now you know what I need you to say tomorrow?

Natalie: Girl, you know I got your back.

Karan: Okay. But just to make sure, I need to go over what you probably need to say tomorrow.

Natalie: Yeah, gotta make sure that I got my lines together.

Karan: Now, you know you need to make sure you say that he raped me.

Natalie: I know.

Karan: And you gotta be good with it, because I'm gonna be good with mine. Yeah, uh-huh . . . Make sure you tell them about how he's never been around my children.

Natalie: Do you think they're going to ask anything about the children?

Karan: You know they will (she laughed). Girl, lemme let you in on something even better: You know that he didn't really do anything—I managed to do it myself with a turkey baster.

Natalie: Shut the fuck up!

Karan: Girl, watch what you're saying around here—I'm tryin' to get paid!

The two friends were having a good time, laughing and joking about setting Dallas up. Karan even promised to pay Natalie $100,000 for her helping her milk the dumb sap out of his money. They even laughed about how Karan bragged how fortunate she was to find that golden condom in the trash can. She ended the conversation joking that she would never have to work another day in her life.

This was definitely the break we needed. Monty more than earned his high fee, and there would definitely be a bonus for his tenacious work.

* * *

Because of Monty's great work, I had to cancel my booty call with Kavion. Sasha and I worked until 2 o'clock in the morning on our motion to dismiss charges against Dallas.

This was clearly an attempt to extort money from my client and if it were not for Monty's discovery we would have had a hard case against us.

Before Ms. Dunn's deposition was to take place, I called Karan Mitchell's attorney and the presiding judge over the case to discuss what transpired last night. I called for the dismissal and after hearing the evidence. The judge agreed.

Chapter 40

Stefan Lewis
Charleston, South Carolina

My attempts at wooing Cole went unnoticed. Reconnecting with Cole was not supposed to be this difficult. My relationship with Cole gave me something to look forward to. I was so in love with Cole that I etched her name on my chest with a knife; I smeared the ink of a red pen over the scars to make it into a permanent tattoo.

Not a day has gone by that I do not wish it were more than a name on my chest. I wanted more. I needed more. The sensation of being in love was euphoric, and I was very happy knowing that we were a couple again after all these years. I had someone real to hold on to every day.

I just wanted Cole to know that we were meant for each other. She's the only person in this God-forsaken world worth living for. If only she could open her eyes and see that her ex-boyfriend cannot protect her the way I can. He can't satisfy her like I do or else she would not be torn between the two of us. He is in the way our togetherness.

It did not take me long to figure out that there was only one solution to my problem. Plain and simple, in fact, he needed to be eliminated. Then Cole would find her way back into my arms.

I just don't know how long I can wait. It's already been eleven years since we were last intimate. Now I know why she hasn't been knocking down my door for a little sampling. She's been giving herself to that other one, that tall, muscular motherfucker.

I cannot go a week let alone a day without seeing her. So, I make sure that I'm out the house by eight just so I can glimpse at her before she heads in to work.

It bothers me that she doesn't return my calls. I don't understand why she would be upset, but women are so moody. So wishy-washy. Doesn't she realize that she would never find someone like me?

Sometimes her ignoring me gets under my skin. But I know what's at stake. Then it dawned on me. I never officially told her I was out of prison. She probably doesn't recognize my voice, so I took the initiative.

"Cole, how are you?' I asked nervously.

"Can I help you with something? I did not catch your name, mister—"

Her response calmed me and she made me feel warm. "I'm surprised you don't remember how I sound. Did you enjoy the flowers I sent you?"

She paused. "Yes, I did. They were quite lovely. Ummm, whom am I speaking to?"

I placed my hand over my chest. I was deeply hurt. "It's me. It's Stefan—"

"Stef . . . Stefan?" she stammered. "How did you get my number? Are you in town?"

I was relieved that she was as excited to hear from me. It was as if my heart had skipped a beat.

"Yes I am. I was hoping we could share dinner tonight? Maybe hang out at the Battery later?" I suggested.

Instead of the response I expected, Cole's reception turned icy on me.

"Stefan, I'm going to ask you very kindly, please do not call me ever again."

I was stupefied. At first, I thought it was because I may have called at a bad time.

"If you ever attempt to call me, I will have your crazy ass arrested before you can wipe it clean. I have you to know if you even attempt to approach me in public, my fiancé will bounce your weird ass around like a basketball. Do I make myself clear?"

She then hung up.

I allowed that to slide and did not bother her again until the next day. Once again, I spoke politely to her.

"Hi, Cole. It's me again. Stefan. Sorry that I upset you. But—"

"Obviously, you do not understand plain English. So since you don't I'm going to make it easy for you."

This time, I hung up.

This was the last straw. I figured that I would give her a final chance, and this would be something I don't usually do. I decided to send her a handwritten letter in which I'd pour out my heart to her.

When I finished, I even scented it with her favorite fragrance. I honestly thought that would do the trick, but it backfired. She never responded. She never took my phone calls. Why would she torture me like this?

The more I thought about it, the more I became enraged. This was now an affront to my manhood.

That bitch, she's nothing but a bitch and a whore!

I retreated to the bathroom and collected my thoughts. I considered picking up my gun and heading over to where I knew she would be. Perhaps brandishing the weapon in front of her would convince her just how much I really love her.

That's right, and in the end she would be in awe and come to her senses.

Damn, somebody would bother me.

"She doesn't love you not even a single bit."

"Yes she does. She'll come running to me," I countered. "Just you wait. Just wait and see."

"I'm telling you, she doesn't love you, fool"

"Yes she does!"

There was a knock on the bathroom door.

"Hey man, are you all right?"

It was my roommate Logan.

"It sounds like you're arguing with someone."

"Uh, yes. I'm on the phone," I yelled through the closed door. "I'll be out in a minute."

I knew that I had to play this off. I went out and made a rare appearance among my younger roommates. The voice in my head laughed at me no sooner than I entered the living room.

Shit!

"You're far too gone to realize you're unstable," he said. "You stopped taking your medicine and all these bright, logical ideas you've been having the past few weeks have abounded. Signs of your slow descent into lunacy. She doesn't love you, you idiot. You're scaring her away."

Chapter 41

Cole Kennedy
Charleston, South Carolina

After lunch, Jabree waltzed into my office and placed the mail on my desk. He reminded me that he had a few things to finish up before he took off for the weekend.

"I have to pick my mother up from the airport this afternoon," he said. "She's coming in at 5:35."

"I hope she has a great time here, Jabree."

"Oh, she will. I've got a lot of things planned for her." He left as quickly as he entered.

I, too, was wrapping up for the day. I had planned to visit Kavion since we did not really spend as much time as I hoped the last time I was in Atlanta.

I found myself grinning when I thought about our conversation from the night before. I felt like I was in college again, all giddy and goofy. My pussy was already drenched just thinking about the next encounter—this has been the happiest she's been in a long time but that's something I'd never confess to Kavion.

On top of the mail was a card. I wondered if it was from one of my clients, but after the most recent events it made me nervous. I opened the envelope; I was not sure if it was Stefan or from the blackmailer. The paper was scented with male cologne.

I'm so disappointed in you, Cole. The last person who hurt me this way is in her grave. Consider this a warning. It's just a matter of time before I find you and when I do . . . let's just say there won't be a second warning.

The message scared me to the core. I could not play around with Stefan any longer. I had no other choice but to call Monty.

Under Monty's instructions, I left the office and took several detours before heading home. All those feelings came back. The fear and the guilt that people died because of me. I could not concentrate not knowing where and when Stefan would pop up. I wondered if he knew where I stayed.

With the advancement of technology, it would not surprise me that anyone from my past could locate me with a click of the mouse. It's a scary world, considering that I could not hide from someone like Stefan, a crazed and delusional stalker.

* * *

Ten years ago, I was forced to testify in the second most traumatic trial of my life. Stefan's stalking terrified me and being in court made me sick to my stomach. The wounds from the prior years had not completely healed. I cried so many nights bemoaning why it happened to me. I had repeated nightmares of him actually getting into my home and hurting or worst, killing me.

I remembered while he was in jail standing trial that he mailed an explicit love letter recounting his love for me. How when he's exonerated from the charges against him that he wanted us to make our relationship legal. He wanted to take our love to the next level. Of course, I gave it to the prosecutor hoping it would strengthen their case.

No matter the reasons, Stefan was a murderer. Someone like him needed psychiatric help. I truly believed he would never be released because during his trial he displayed classic psychotic behavior. He insisted to the judge who saw him during the sentencing that there was nothing wrong with him. He then threatened everyone who had been involved in the case against him. There was no way any court would release him back into our society. I was wrong.

My worst nightmare came true when I received a call from Stefan unexpectedly. He wanted to take me out to dinner and then a late-night stroll overlooking the bridge.

Wow. Sydney Starks, the ex-con and Madame, and Stefan, the psychopath and killer. Somehow, both have weaseled their way back into my life. I could not handle this alone and with Kavion being over three hundred miles away.

Monty's phone call was the best thing I heard once I got home, having been so frazzled.

"Trust no one you don't know," Monty instructed me.

"Good, I start acting silly when I'm paranoid."

"Don't feel silly. Paranoid is good."

Great, I thought to myself.

"Do you have a security system?"

"Well no, I didn't think I needed one." I looked around my home. Although I lived on the sixth floor, I guess there were opportunities if he knew how to scale walls. Or swing from a rope. Shaking my head, paranoia had turned me in to a crazy person.

I worked with Monty long enough to know that he was resourceful and well informed. Although I was freaked out, there was a sense of relief after we conversed. He was able to give me the 4-1-1 on Stefan: How he had been released from the mental ward over a year ago. He had completed his probation two months ago and was free to live his life as he pleased. He was encouraged to maintain a relationship with a therapist when things got complicated, but it was not required.

What was so alarming was that Stefan told his halfway housemates that he and I were planning to get married. Somebody this crazy should not have been released. More importantly, however, the authorities should have notified me of his release.

"Cole, I want you to do this for me," Monty suggested. "Call me once you get to your boyfriend's house since this Stefan fella sent you that threatening letter, okay?"

"Okay, I'll do that. Do you suggest that I get myself a gun?"

"It wouldn't hurt, but I don't recommend it without proper firearms training."

This was getting the best of me. "Monty, once again in my life I feel I'm being forced to relive another bad dream."

"Don't worry. I have my boys working on a few things. If we can find him, I'm going to show him what it feels like to stalk and harass someone. But in the meantime, I want you to stay away from your home until I tell you its safe."

"All right, I'll call you once I arrive at Kavion's house."

After I hung up the phone with Monty, I called Kavion's cell phone; there was no answer. I tried his house phone. No answer there. Then I tried his cell phone again. No answer.

I was still intent on leaving for the airport. I was scheduled to arrive at his Decatur home in less than four hours.

Chapter 42

Stefan Lewis
Decatur, Georgia

I felt like the Joker all day. I was so giddy that all things could very well come together, and they did.

The look in her eyes were worth everything that I sacrificed in my life for her.

"How are you?" I greeted Cole the moment she walked inside.

I had every reason to believe that she was happy to see me as I was seeing her. Just as she was about to scream, I rushed to cover her mouth with my hand so that she would not alarm any of the neighbors.

Her eyes told me she understood as I signaled her to hush. So I released my hold and pointed to the chair near the window. I followed her to the chair, checking the windows and drawing the curtains extra tight.

"What are you doing here?" she mumbled; her eyes then scanned the living room. "Where is Kavion?"

What a glorious moment. He was always a non-factor and today proved it. "It's okay," I reasoned with her. "We do not have to hide anymore. Everyone is jealous because we have something special. Something they wish they had. Cole, I can't let them be the reason for keeping us apart."

I bent over and kissed her forehead, but she jerked her head away.

"Stefan, please tell me what is going on here?"

Pity. It sounded as if she's been brainwashed. That funky attitude began reappearing. If it now meant going to my grave with it, I'd never share with her how I timed it so perfectly being here to greet her.

I spoke calmly to her. "I'm here to take you away with me. We can finally be together again. I do not care where we go just as long as I am with you."

"Tell me when did I ever give you the impression that I would go anywhere with you?" she retorted; her tone was belligerent to me.

"Maybe it was my idea—"

"No, it was your fantasy."

"You can't deny you have feelings for me." I tried to diffuse the aggression in her voice. If she can only admit to herself that I am the man for her.

"I only have feelings for Kavion, not you. It will never be you!" she yelled.

I stood there and marveled at her. The beauty. The feistiness. The vaunted professionalism. I chortled and shook my head because she had failed to recognize that she began to annoy me. There was no way she would put a damper on my high-risk move that yielded such a high-risk reward by being in her immediate presence.

I figured maybe if she could see that Kavion Cottrell was far from the man she thought he was then she would see that he's not enough man for her. How can he protect her when he's tied to a chair along with two of his friends in the basement? What if a burglar snuck in his home while she was here? What if he wanted to hurt Cole? How would Kavion defend her?

It was apparent that she needed some convincing. So, I led her downstairs to a half-finished basement. When we turned the corner, I flipped the light switch on. The three scumbags were still tied to their chairs just as I left them. Kavion's eyes widened when he saw the gun I brandished with Cole in front of me. This was a righteous cause of having suffered relational violence and the violent needing to take things by force.

"It could have been different if you had let nature take its course. But no, you had to interfere in between what I and Cole had." I then stepped towards Kavion. "I love her more than anything in the world and you tried to take her from me."

I reached for Cole's hand and jerked her to me. I wanted her to be up close, and I wanted her to see Kavion the way I saw him: He was a loser like all the other jocks in this God-forsaken world. He never had the balls to stand up and defend the woman he claimed he loved. He could barely protect himself. How else was I able to bring down him and his two goons to their knees?

"We will be together with or without you," I said, raising the gun to Kavion's temple. "I wish it did not have to end this way."

"Stefan, think about what you are doing," Cole cried out. "Please don't shoot him."

I wished she had fought this hard for our love. "Cole, I've thought about this for two months. Ever since I saw you and Kavion in Charleston."

"What are you talking about?"

She reacted as expected, even with her hand trembling in mine. So I elaborated further.

"You have to remember that night. It was the night you broke my heart. I witnessed it with my own eyes. After Charleston's Best Gala, you should have been in my arms but instead you returned to his hotel suite. The receptionist said you were his wife. You had to have known that really hurt.

"These past two months, I convinced myself that you were only playing house until I came back home. Well, I'm home, damnit. You don't have to pretend any more. We can be together. There will be no one standing in between our happiness."

Then I cocked the gun and aimed it near Kavion's chest.

"Nooooo!" she screamed.

She then did something I would have never imagined. She tackled me to the ground just as the gun went off. It was not a wasted bullet, however. It did not hit the intended target, but it hit one of his friends. His head snapped back, knocking him flat on his back. He lay motionless on the floor.

Humph, fuck him.

Next, she scrambled off me and in the direction of the gun. She was quick, but I grabbed her by the foot and pulled her back towards me. Her fingers were just inches away from the butt of the gun.

"Now why did you do that?" I demanded.

There was no way I would allow such disrespect. Nor would I have acted that way towards another female. It was supposed to be us against the fucking world.

In the midst of the commotion, I thought fast and straddled her body; both of us still fought for the gun. She was a feisty bitch, clawing and kicking out of control. Because I was on top, I had the upper hand. I slapped her across the cheek; her face quickly bruised. She also calmed for a second.

It hurt to hit her, but she gave me no choice. I pinned her easily with one hand and grabbed hold of the gun with the other. Then I did it without thinking. I knocked her out with the butt of the gun. Maybe I wanted to punish her for disrespecting me—I did not know where it came from. But it sure as hell felt good.

Kavion's muffles interrupted me.

"Damn, when will you get it through your damn head that she doesn't want to be with you?" I said, sneering at him. "She had already confided in me that she was only here to break things off with you, and she realized that she made a big mistake. "

Just like a scene in the movies, his eyes widened again and he cursed at me while he struggled to free himself from the chair. His pitiful defiance merely motivated me to cut him straight to the heart with the truth.

"Why else would she plan to run away with me, dumb ass? I forgave her for fucking around," I said. "She admitted that she was caught up in dating a celebrity.

"That was yesterday. Today is a new day and a new life. A new life with the love of her life."

I gently picked up Cole in my arms. For a split second, I envisioned our wedding day as I carried her through the threshold of our island retreat. In our moment of consummation, I'd lay her carefully on the king size bed, peel away her delicate gown off her sun-kissed skin before making sweet, passionate love to her.

Before Kavion, however, I kissed her softly on the lips. I could taste the cinnamon from her breath. She excited me. She always did.

From the first moment I saw her, Cole always stoked my loins like no other woman was ever capable of doing. Not even Fiona, and that meant a lot because Fiona was my first true love. Cole was different. She was special. Being with Cole allowed me to be free. I no longer felt suffocation, and I never wanted this feeling of euphoria to disappear. Even if that meant eliminating my enemies by any means necessary.

She may not agree with the methods. Sometimes I stump myself, but I accepted the fact that love may be hazardous to one's health.

"Look at what you made me do." I yelled at the top of my lungs, raising the gun above his head. "This is all your fucking fault!"

In the next motion, I reared back and struck Kavion on the temple with so much force that it sliced into my flesh. Immediately, he slumped in the chair and he was out cold. A thin trail of drool escaped from his lips and made a small puddle on his shirt. I shook my head at the pitiful sight.

Humph, fuck him, too!

And to think, she actually contemplated leaving me for his sorry ass? I was glad she came to her senses because she would have no doubt been disappointed when it counted the most.

I walked out the basement more confused than before. It was not supposed to be like this. By now, Cole and I should have rekindled our love. We should have been on our way to paradise. I had already found a deal on the Internet and bought two tickets to a private beach in the Turks and Caicos Islands. The travel agent had actually told me that this was where real lovers go for fun and relaxation.

Chapter 43

Cole Kennedy
Decatur, Georgia

I reached or at least tried touching my throbbing head, but my hands were bound together.

My left eye was swollen shut, and I could barely see past the blurred vision out of my right eye. I felt helpless. All I could think about was how I didn't want to die this way.

Suddenly, there was movement across the room; it startled me and I screamed out of fear.

This was hardly what I wanted to see. I looked up at Stefan's smiling, deranged face. He tried smoothing my hair down as a mother would to her sick child.

"You took a nasty blow to the head. We were worried about you, but you'll live."

My voice cracked, but I asked Stefan calmly about his plans.

"It was my plan to take you away from all this madness," he said. "I bought two plane tickets to Turks and Caicos, and I rented a nice home off the waters just for you and only for you."

"Why would you do that?"

"For LOVE!" He got up and started hitting himself in the head. I had to think of something.

"I'm glad to have someone like you looking out for me. I'm glad to have someone like you in my life—"

The look in his face suggested that I was on the right path. I waited, blinking my one good eye. I fiercely tried to blink it into focus.

I stumbled with my words, but I hoped they were effective. "I don't know what came over me. I . . . I should not have disrespected you. I'm sorry."

He rushed to the other side of the bed and faced me. There was an awkward glow to his face.

"Cole, you just don't know how long I've waited for you to come back to me. If we leave here by eight, we can still catch our flight."

This motherfucker was serious. Now I really had to think of something fast, or I might end up another pretty face lost abroad.

"I can't leave looking like this," I said. "My eye feels like it is as big as a grapefruit. The authorities would surely believe you hit me."

"It's not as bad as you think, honey. With some sun glasses, you can walk out of here looking like a movie star."

His callous touch scraped across my cheek. If I did not know better, I would have thought he touched me with a pocketknife. I contained the urge to flinch. How could someone as beautiful as he be a nutty time bomb?

"Ummm sweetie, I would like to freshen up before we leave. Do you mind?"

I held up my bound hands. I prayed he would unleash their hold, which he did.

"But you do know that you're beautiful. You've always been beautiful in my eyes."

"Stefan, I really think this is necessary. Besides, I need to use the ladies' room."

I made sure that I was in the bathroom before I posed the next question I had for him. I hoped that he would not be angry and go off the deep end with it.

"Stefan, my love," I shouted from behind the locked door. "Is Kavion and his friends still alive? Because we cannot start our lives together as fugitives. That's no way to live."

Chapter 44

Kavion Cottrell
Decatur, Georgia

I woke up about the same time my teammate Ryker was removing the duct tape from around his ankles. His head was covered in dried blood.

"That bullet grazed my temple. I'm a little woozy, but I'll live," he joked.

I directed him to the toolbox as I remembered I had a box cutter beneath shit that I never used. While he quietly searched the toolbox I kept a lookout. The house felt still when he returned with the blade.

"Did you hear anything? Do you know if Cole is okay?" I asked; the alarm in my voice was evident. "I don't know what I'd do if that punk ass Stefan has hurt her."

I was determined not to lose her a second time. Not to stupidity and surely not by some stalker lunatic. Stefan had fucked with the wrong man this time.

"I thought I heard him carrying Cole upstairs," Ryker said.

Meanwhile, he tiptoed towards me and cut through the duct tape that bound my legs and wrists to the chair. And Preston was still knocked out; I did not know when that crazy motherfucker might decide to come back and use that .38 on us.

"I need you to help Preston out of here while I find Cole," I said.

"Uh-uh. That motherfucker shot me in the head! That shit almost killed me. If it's the last thing I do, I'm getting a piece of his ass," Ryker snarled.

Ryker walked over to our teammate Preston and slapped him lightly on the face while I removed the tape from around my wrists and then my legs.

"Preston wake up," he whispered.

I searched around the basement for some type of weapon to use on this sick fuck. All of my guns were on the main and second floors. I prayed he did not find them even if they were inside special thumbprint recognition cases. I found an old set of golf clubs, a sledgehammer, and a wooden bat.

Preston finally came to. He was a little discombobulated. I asked him if he was okay, but I still wanted him to get his bearings before he went for help.

"I think that motherfucker is still here with Cole," he said, rather groggy.

I told him that Ryker and I were going after him.

"Just give me a few minutes." He rubbed his throbbing head. The brunt force of the gun gave each of us matching knots aside our heads.

It was embarrassing that a prick like Stefan Lewis was able to control three athletes such as ourselves. He pretended to be from the gas company checking for leaks, but then he pulled out a gun and forced me on my knees. I thought it was a home evasion gone wrong.

When I came to from the jolt of the stun gun, I was downstairs in my basement and duct-taped to a poker chair. If I had anything to do with it, that story would never go public. I felt all we had to do now was get to my home office adjacent to the foyer where I kept a .44 magnum in the drawer of my desk. It was dark outside but the moon shone through the skylight to give us just enough light to see our way to the office without bumping into any furniture. Since I had only one gun down stairs, I gave Ryker the driver club from my titanium golf set.

"I don't need this shit." Ryker had barely kept his voice low. "When I see that little fucker, I'm going to stump a mud hole in his ass. "

Ryker, who's slightly shorter than me at five-eleven and two hundred and fifty pounds, had a look on him that reminded me of our playoff game last season. In the huddle, he said he was determined to take the other team's best player, a running back, out of the game. He did, with a ferocious tackle; the running back needed two players to help him off the field and he never returned. I was sure he felt as if he was ran over by a Mack truck.

I heard movement from the far end of the house. It sounded as though they were in one of the upstairs guest rooms. I signaled Ryker to follow my lead. I was planning on a sneak attack, but Ryker had a plan of his own.

"Fuck that," he said.

Ryker managed to be light-footed while he ran up the stairs, and I was quick to follow. The door was closed, but there were muffled voices coming from the other side. I could hear Stefan speaking to Cole; however, I did not hear her respond.

I could not finish my count to three before Ryker had already kicked the door down off one of the hinges. Stefan twirled around fast. His eyes were widened like a horror movie victim and the gun shook in his hand. The larger gun I pointed in his direction had his attention.

"Put it down, cowboy." I said, eager to pull the trigger.

Stefan smiled a wicked smile before he responded, "I sent her out of her misery."

I didn't want to believe that, so I called out Cole's name. There was no response.

"Where is she, motherfucker. Or I'll put a bullet through your sick skull."

Ryker used the distraction as his opportunity to disarm Stefan. He threw the golf club at him like a spear, knocking the gun from Stefan's grip. Before I realized it, Ryker had already tackled Stefan to the floor and commenced to whipping his ass.

"Go find Cole. I can handle this." Ryker said, having straddled the fool and pummeled him into unconsciousness.

I checked the bathroom adjoining the guest room. The window was open. I was afraid to look out of it; however, I saw where Cole had fallen down the two floors. She lied there motionless and did not respond to my calling her name.

I charged down the stairs and outside the house. I heard the police siren in the distance. Great, I thought to myself, Preston was able to contact the authorities.

By the time I reached Cole, she was trying to get up but the pain in her leg kept her on her plump ass.

"The bushes broke my fall, but I think my leg's broken," she said.

The next thing I heard was a gun shot from inside the house. It shook both of us.

I ran back inside, up the stairs, and to the guest room. It appeared that Preston had come to Ryker's rescue.

"I shot that bitch just as he stabbed Ryker," Preston said.

Ryker sat upright on the floor with the knife still lodged in his abdomen. He was losing a lot of blood. I grabbed a towel and pressed firmly against his wound.

"Preston, bring the cops up here and make sure someone helps Cole. She fell out the window and she has a broken leg," I yelled. "We need an ambulance, fast."

I turned my attention to Ryker. It was not looking good for him. He appeared to be falling in and out of consciousness.

"Man, I need you to hang in there," I pleaded to my friend.

Then I turned my attention to the lifeless body of Stefan. If it wasn't for the fact he was already dead with a bullet wound to his chest, I would have given him one good punch in the jaw and a kick to the groin. He had put Cole and my friends through one hell of a ride.

Fortunately, the EMS responded quickly. I moved out of the way so that they could attend to Ryker. They needed to stop the bleeding. They moved fast and efficient and in less than ten minutes, they had my friend strapped to the gurney and were carrying him down the stairs. They informed me they were taking him to the nearest hospital.

I finished my initial interview with the detectives. I told them how Stefan Lewis pretended to be a representative from the gas company and he was there to investigate a gas leak.

"He seemed to be legitimate. He had a company uniform on, a note pad, and some equipment with him," I said.

"What happened after that?" I was asked by a detective, who introduced himself as Gerard Strong.

"I showed him to the basement. The gas meter is just outside of it. When I turned around, he pointed a gun at me."

I told the detective that my teammate Ryker and my fiancée Cole were also hurt and I needed to be at the hospital. I collected the business card from Detective Strong and promised I would meet them the next day if they needed any other information.

Afterward, I ran into Preston outside the front door. Since we gave pretty much of the same account, the detectives released Preston and, of course, warned him not to leave town since the case was ongoing.

"They just took her to General Hospital, same place as Ryker. My car is not blocked in so I can drive," he said.

For someone who just shot down an assailant dead, he seemed unfazed. I told him I preferred to drive, so I snatched the keys from his hand.

We got to the hospital in record time. After some nervous hours spent, we were informed that Ryker survived surgery that was performed by Dr. Frasier Kennard, a specialist who was called on his day off. It turned out that he did not mind since Ryker was his son's favorite football player. He informed us that Ryker had suffered a stab wound that missed puncturing his kidney by less than two centimeters.

Cole suffered a broken tibia and several bruised ribs. The day after she was released, we checked into the Ritz-Carlton Hotel and spent an entire month.

I told her I wanted her to feel safe and that I would always be there to protect her. I spoiled her with room service, dining out, and spa treatments. I pampered her like royalty, and I wanted her to know that I was her lover and best friend.

Chapter 45

Cole Kennedy
Atlanta, Georgia

To say the least, the past month was crazier than I could have ever imagined. Since I've been an advocate for victim's rights, I followed my own advice and immediately sought counseling after my nightmarish episode with Stefan—who wouldn't?

Three other people were put in a life-or-death situation all because I was the object of a delusional stalker's infatuations. I felt somewhat responsible for Kavion and his friends' ordeal—who wouldn't?

It's taken much for me to understand that I was not to blame for Stefan's behavior. I've had to learn that stalkers tend to become violent the more they're warped by their delusions.

What's also particularly important is the victim's circle of support, particularly emotional. With Kavion's insistence, I decided to take his offer to be my personal caretaker, and I did just that by taking some time off from the practice. I called my office and told them a condensed version of the facts, and that I would stay in Atlanta while I recuperated from my broken leg.

When I first attended my sessions, Kavion would escort me to the office but then he'd retreat to his car until my session ended. Eventually, he took note to how my spirits were lifted and I no longer acted as a victim. What I needed most of all was that assurance that I had no control over another person's actions. Kavion eventually surprised me by joining me on my last few sessions. It helped strengthen our bond to one another.

After a month at the Ritz-Carlton, I convinced Kavion that we should return to his home. I felt he had spent enough money on that luxury suite.

"No amount of money is too much for my baby," he said.

He then took me in his arms. I was mesmerized by his adoring looks.

"Cole, I want to spend the rest of my life with you. I don't care if it's in Timbuktu. If you're ready to return home to Charleston, I will follow you there."

"Kavion, I can't let you throw away your career. You know as well as I that you are fortunate to have had a successful career as long as you have."

I still needed my crutch for balance, so he held me up and I dared him to let me fall.

"I would rather walk away with the woman I love and on top of my game than to let you slip through my fingers again. Nothing else matters." He kissed me softly on the lips. Then he sat me down on the plush chocolate color sectional. He retreated to the dining area where I heard him fumbling around for something. I called out to see if he needed a hand.

"Nope, I have everything under control," he responded.

After several moments passed, I heard a pop from what appeared to be the cork from the champagne bottle. He soon returned with two glasses filled with the Armand de Brignac.

"Cole I have big plans for us." He pulled out a small black velvety box from his trousers and got down on one knee. I had no idea he was thinking marriage. Tears welled up and blurred my vision. So I put the glass on the coffee table. My heart pounded so fast that I thought I would hyperventilate.

"Cole, you have always been my true love, my only love. I thought I lost you, but destiny brought us together again. When it feels right, you have to go with your heart and my heart, my soul, wants you forever in my life." His voice cracked and then he cleared his throat. He opened the ring box revealing a three-carat diamond princess cut ring; it was gorgeous.

"Cole Kennedy, will you do me the honor by becoming my wife?"

I jumped up so fast that I practically tackled him. I kissed him passionately and whispered "yes." I extended my hand so that he could place the biggest and prettiest ring I'd ever seen on my finger.

We spent the remainder of the night enjoying each other's bodies. It was awkward trying to strip tease with a full leg cast. We both laughed when I lost my balance and stumbled back onto the bed.

So sexy, right?

Kavion took over and gently removed my clothing. He still had a way of making me nervous. And the fact that this would be the first time we made love since that fateful night with Stefan, it made me even more nervous.

"I never thought we'd ever have a moment like this again," I whispered to him.

"I guess love cannot be denied. It is a great force, a magnifying force. This is a virtue of love's power—"

He repositioned me on the bed, propping pillows around me to make my leg comfortable given my lack of mobility and flexibility.

I sat there admiring him as he set the mood. First, he turned on the Bose system to some midnight jam playlist. The smooth sounds of Babyface "Whip Appeal" filled the suite. I could hear him in the background singing.

The thoughts of someone cooking dinner for me once I returned home from work resonated deeply within me. It had been amazing having someone wait on me hand and foot who also knew how to take special care of my pleasure spots in between.

Kavion returned from the living room with the glasses and bottle of champagne. I sipped on the champagne while he began rubbing my feet. I relaxed and closed my eyes.

"Mmm . . . don't stop, don't ever stop," I whispered.

Damn if he didn't . . . he stopped. Yet it was only for a second. I felt a wet trail of kisses ascend along my inner thighs to my pussy. Yes, his head was buried inside my goodies.

"Kavion," I gasped.

He did not let up, nor did I. Everything that had been pent up in me went out the door, so to speak, and there was neither guilt nor sorrow. The anxiety dissipated. Although Stefan would never be a threat to me, I couldn't help shake the feeling he was still watching me.

The fear was temporary, however. Kavion's tongue flicked in and out my slit. I responded to him by moving my hips up, down, and around to his rhythm.

"Ahh shit," I moaned, caressing his head.

He looked up at me; his face glistened from my arousal. "You like that?" He resumed sucking my clit.

"Oh yesss!" I hissed before the room began spinning around.

I tried desperately to move away, but he held my hips and made sure my mound was pressed to his lips. I begged him to stop. He was not hearing me.

Everything that held me down had released in a major way. It felt great. I felt like a new woman. And I was still euphoric from Kavion's proposal.

Just the thought of becoming Mrs. Cole Kennedy-Cottrell excited me as much as his dick filling me entirely.

After our moment of intimacy, we retired in the California king size bed in each other's arms feeding each other fresh fruit as we talked about our lives together.

"I was thinking I could set up an office here in the Atlanta-area," I posed to him. "Of course, I would have to convince the executive committee to approve my proposal. Since winning Dallas case, I've had more potential clients than I could ever handle."

I mentioned to him that our firm was recognized as one of the nation's most notable law firms. There would be no reason why my firm would not want to expand. It would just be adding another office.

"I would keep it small," I went on to explain. "I would need Jabree, a receptionist, and two paralegals to keep it efficient. In addition, if business becomes too overwhelming, I could ask for a couple of associates to help with the caseloads."

I was almost positive I had the perfect plan.

"You know I'll support you. I know plenty of players that could use your skills when it comes to the court of law." He laughed, but his comments rang true. Dallas had already sent three of his friends to see me.

"Speaking of sports, I was offered a position on a new entertainment show and I'm seriously considering the offer. The pay isn't bad, either."

"Are you serious?" I reacted. "When did this happen?"

I was so happy for him that I ended up on top of him and smothering him with kisses.

Life was great again, albeit a little crazier and busier than before.

Since we were making a new life together, Kavion called his realtor. He felt like we should at least start fresh in a new home, our home.

The next morning, I woke up to a tray of a light breakfast: scrambled eggs, turkey bacon, coffee and a vase with a single red rose. He also left a note that he had an early meeting with producers from CNN and he would return in a couple of hours.

I made some phone calls and left messages for Autry Brown, Jabree, and Monty.

Monty was the first to return any of my calls.

"Do you have a fax machine nearby?"

"Yes I do."

I found the number of the fax machine in the executive office in the suite.

"I've been working hard trying to uncover the UNSUB behind the blackmail. Yesterday, I spoke with the PI in San Diego, Albert Shaw, in detail. I went out on a limb and got lucky. I'm sending the fax now; call me as soon as you receive my report."

Before we hung up, Monty asked about my leg and we talked about my plans to practice in the Atlanta-Metro area, my engagement to Kavion, and how I was coping with the ordeal with Stefan.

"Hey, I'll keep in touch," he said.

"I'm sure you will, Monty." I still had to find a way to approach him about working solely for me.

The fax beeped, indicating the transmission had finished. I was eager to find out the person who wanted to blackmail me. I had flipped through eight of ten pages from Monty's report when I discovered the identity of the individual who thought I'd be silly enough to un-ass fifty thousand and possibly more down the line.

The photo was a grainy black-n-white, but there was no mistaking who was behind it all. I would have never believed someone could stoop so low. The hard, icy glare and whose face had been hardened by time and circumstance that stared back at me was familiar: Sydney Starks.

I laughed at the insanity of her ploy. Then I took action. I made a few calls to California, and within two weeks she was arrested for violating her parole plus additional charges of blackmail and extortion.